D1189969

ALL YOU CAN EAT

A BUFFET OF LESBIAN
ROMANCE & EROTICA

R.G. EMANUELLE
ANDI MARQUETTE
EDITORS

Sign up for our newsletter to hear about new releases,
read interviews with authors, enter giveaways, and more.

http://www.ylva-publishing.com

M ENU

INTRODUCTION

Great food is like great sex. The more
you have the more you want.

—*Gael Greene*

THIS ANTHOLOGY, LIKE STRONG COFFEE, percolated for a while before we decided to serve it up. The two of us co-edited an earlier anthology—*Skulls and Crossbones: Tales of Women Pirates* (2010)—and we had so much fun putting it together that we planned to do another at some point in the future.

We pondered quite a few options, and then it hit us. We decided to work with a theme that both of us love and that at least one of us has a whole lot of experience with. R.G. Emanuelle is a long-time foodie, food writer, and culinary school graduate while Andi just really likes food and all the things it signals about life and love.

So we decided to put our different perspectives to work and explore the sensuous qualities of food and how the act of preparing and eating it can engage all the senses, not just taste and smell. To do this, we planned a menu that includes a variety of authors who incorporated food, romance, and erotica into their stories. We purposely left the subject open-ended so contributors could roam freely through time and place and bring their own particular tastes to the table. We

1

required only that the story must incorporate food in its romantic and/or erotic trajectory. And in order to stay true to the different flavors around the world, we've kept the authors' international spellings intact.

Readers will find that each story also ends with a recipe. Some of these require cooking implements while others are whimsical accompaniments that don't require cooking at all—at least not in the traditional sense. We then arranged the menu like a sumptuous meal by heat level, from warm, romantic appetizers to smoldering entrées that build to even hotter desserts.

With that in mind, our appetizer selections—delectable bits to prime your palate for the next courses—include Ashley Bartlett, who in "Fresh Fruit" takes us on an urban tour of publicly available fruit and shows us how the quest for it can lead to much more than free food. A bit of lust and longing flavors the historical setting of Historia's "The Luscious *Tarte Aux Fraises*," in which a woman wishes to sample the wares of another of the fairer sex.

Jae then brings us in "Whining and Dining" a woman who is so focused on preparing a meal for a future date with the help of her chef friend that she nearly misses what she has right in front of her. And finally, Rebekah Weatherspoon re-ignites a struggling connection in a longstanding relationship through a heartfelt meal in "Burn."

Our entrée selections turn the heat up. Some cook with a slow burn while others go right to boil. We start in Australia at a grower's market, where Cheyenne Blue introduces us to the "Tomato Lady," the catalyst for a romance. Karis Walsh adds Indian spice with a Texas twist in "East Meets West," in which a woman from Assam wonders if a San Antonio cowgirl could be the right recipe for her.

In "Dessert Platter," Victoria Oldham demonstrates that, sometimes, food isn't just on the menu; it can instead be on a woman willing to test her boundaries and experiment with a partner's fantasy. Cheri Crystal's "Appetizing" shows readers that a deli counter can tantalize much more than taste buds, while Andi Marquette cooks up a hot Southern summer night with old friends who discover something new in "Sugar and 'Shine."

Our dessert menu includes savory and seductive selections, some of which definitely turn the oven to high. For your first dessert, Jove Belle provides a cake-baking lesson two women won't soon forget in "Vanilla Extract." Art and food collide in wholly unexpected ways when an artist asks a food critic to be part of her next installation in R.G. Emanuelle's "Smorgasbord." Sacchi Green doesn't need a torch for her "Crème Brûlée"—a hot butch and an ex-lover manage to scorch a picnic table near Provincetown without one. Finishing out our desserts is Yvonne Heidt's "Turn the Tables," an erotic ode to ancient Rome, in which a female gladiator and her noblewoman patron engage in much more than a meal.

We hope you enjoy the menu, and that reading the selections leads to some cooking of your own, whether in or out of the kitchen. And we hope, ultimately, that you find, as we have, that food is sexy.

R.G. Emanuelle
Andi Marquette
2014

APPETIZERS

FRESH FRUIT

ASHLEY BARTLETT

THE TREE WASN'T VERY TALL. Perfect height, really. It was mine, which was the problem. I could have gone for another tree, another orange. But somehow, I knew that those oranges would taste better. As if working for it made it better than its closer, more available counterparts.

Or maybe it was just the bitch who owned the tree.

That was the real issue. Maybe at one time she had owned the whole thing, but it had grown and stretched and spread. The roots had buckled the sidewalk—not a lot—just enough so you'd know they were there. The limbs sprawled flirtatiously over the heads of passersby. Who cared if the trunk was behind a fence? I figured enough of it was public property. That made it fair game, right?

Of course, the bitch was also aware of the sketchy ownership issue. So she picked every goddamn orange in reach. I didn't know when she did it. Before the sun was up. I'd started checking in the afternoons. Then mornings. Three a.m. Six p.m. Each week I would choose a couple oranges and watch them. Just when one had a week to go before it was perfect, the damn thing would disappear. That really pissed me off. She picked them before they were ripe, so she wasn't even enjoying them.

There was an alley that ran behind her house and continued across the street. That was where I watched. In a non-stalker sort of way. Really. I just leaned against a fence at the mouth of the alley and scoped out the tree. I studied the distance from fence to orange. Maybe I could vault up and grab one. Or maybe just take a running jump. I could grab the top of the fence and haul myself up, but that seemed like cheating. It was on public property so I had to use only public property to reach it.

As I stood there, eating pilfered figs from two streets back and one over, I gradually became aware that someone was standing behind me. Very close. I turned and found either a very pretty boy or a very handsome girl. Hard to tell in the dusky light.

"What are you doing?" she asked. The voice gave it away.

"It depends."

"On what?" She was already reaching for her back pocket. Cell phone probably. Police? That would be fun to explain.

"If you like figs." I held out a sticky handful.

"What's wrong with you?" Her hand dropped back to her side. Not getting arrested over an orange tree. Good thing.

"That's kind of a big question. You live around here?"

"Yes." She crossed her arms and hit me with a fantastic stare. "No. My mom does." She nodded at the house I was standing next to. I'd figured I was short enough that the occupants couldn't see me. But now I clearly looked like a creeper.

"I go on fruit walks. I promise I'm not doing anything weird." I shrugged.

"Fruit walks?" She definitely thought I was insane.

"It's this thing. This art movement. Like a fruit map. Never mind. I walk around and pick fruit that's growing on public property."

"You're serious right now," she said.

"Well, yeah. It's great for when friends come into town. I've mapped out where all the avocado and lime trees are. Guacamole, you know. Or I just go out when I'm bored or hungry. There are bananas in an alley about six blocks that way." I nodded up the street. "And there's a pomegranate tree a couple blocks up from there."

"You walk around and pick fruit?"

"Well, uh, yeah."

"You hard up for cash?"

"No. I don't know. It's organic. I guess it's like a statement. Cutting out the corporate farm, mass supermarket bullshit. Plus, it's fun." I took a bite and offered her one.

"I don't like figs."

"Okay. How do you feel about peaches?" I opened the bag slung over my shoulder. I had two peaches, some bananas, and a plantain. The plantain was iffy. I was pretty sure those weren't supposed to grow in SoCal. But my brother had just emailed me a fried plantain recipe and dared me to go for it.

She gave me a hard stare, then reached into the open bag. She lifted the peach, but stopped halfway to her mouth. "Are you the one who's been cutting my mom's irises?"

"Irises?" I peeked around the corner. The house was fronted with a line of cultivated flowers. Half the irises were sliced right off. "No, man. That's not cool. Everyone can enjoy flowers. Why would you cut them?"

She shook her head. I guess I could see the jump there. Fruit to flowers. She took a bite. Her eyebrow went up as she chewed slowly and swallowed. A line of juice trailed down her chin. She wiped it with the cuff of her shirt.

"This is amazing."

9

"Fresh."

"Well, yeah. I guess so." She nodded. Girl was on board. "Still doesn't explain why you're creeping around my mom's back fence."

"Oh, that. See the tree across the street?" She took another bite and nodded for me to continue. "Well, it grows these awesome-looking oranges. But the chick who owns it picks them before they're ripe. I'm pretty sure she just chucks them."

She started laughing. "Yeah. That's Marion. Total bitch. I can see her doing that."

"I should probably let it go. But it's just so wrong. I mean, why not let people eat them? It's the principle of the thing. I have to get one of those oranges."

"All of that made sense. I'm now concerned."

"Why?"

"Because I'm following your logic. And I'm not sure how sane you are. Which means I'm crazy."

"Nah. It's weird, but it's not insane. I promise," I said.

"I've never noticed any fruit trees around here."

"You weren't looking for them. Check it out." I pulled a worn section of a map from my pocket. It was a fifteen-block radius around my apartment. I'd drawn colored dots for each kind of fruit. She took another bite of peach and leaned close to look.

"What's this?" She pointed to a series of blue dots two streets over.

"Avocado."

"I walk past there every day. There's no avocado trees there."

"You gotta look up."

She took another bite of peach, sucked on it, swallowed. "Show me."

"Yeah?"

"Yeah. Show me."

"Let's go." Maybe that wasn't smart. Maybe she wasn't the one who should be concerned. I didn't know her. But she was hot and she smelled like fresh peaches.

"I'll be right back." She took the steps up to her mom's house two at a time and opened the door. "Hey, Ma. I'll be back." There was a muffled yell from inside the house. "No, she won't bother you anymore."

I shuffled my feet. Christ, I'd been scaring an old lady. I kinda felt like a jerk.

She jumped back down the stairs.

"Sorry if I freaked your mom out. I didn't realize anyone could see me."

"No big. She's pissed about the flowers is all."

We took our time walking. She kept pace when I cut up the right street. I stopped in the middle of the sidewalk and looked up. There were two small avocados in easy reach. I kept searching.

"So where are they?" she asked.

"Look up."

"Holy shit."

There were two trees. One was rooted next to an apartment building. It was so high, you'd have to lean out of the windows to snag the fruit. The second tree was in the strip of grass between the sidewalk and the street. The branches were just low enough to touch.

"So how do you pick 'em?"

I shrugged. "Find a couple good ones and see if you can reach."

We spent a few minutes scoping the tree before deciding that the small ones were the only fruit in reach. There were a couple dark, good-sized avocados about a foot above our fingertips. Which was annoying.

"Do we climb?" she asked.

I sized her up. "How good is your balance?"

"What do you mean?"

I laced my fingers together and held my hands out low. "Just use my shoulders for balance."

"You've done this before?"

"My big sister was a cheerleader. My brother and I were forced to help her practice." Mom had paid us five bucks an hour. Not a bad gig. At fifteen. We wised up quick.

"If I fall, I'm gonna punch you."

"Noted."

She put her foot in my hand and braced herself on my shoulder. "You ready?"

"On three, hop up. One, two, three."

She jumped and leaned against me. Her thigh pressed against my shoulder. Rough denim brushed my cheek. This was way better than helping my sister with cheerleading practice.

"I've almost got it. Can you go to the right a little?"

I staggered to the side. She grabbed a branch to balance herself.

"Did you get it?"

"How many do we want?"

"I don't know. Two?"

"Okay. Got 'em," she said.

"Cool. I'm gonna let you go. Ready?"

"Yeah." She dropped and handed me two perfect avocados. "Now what?"

"I don't know. Lime?" I tucked the avocados into my bag.

"You want to make guac?"

"I make awesome guac," I said. "And I've got Modelo in my fridge."

"I'm in. But only for the Modelo." She pulled the map out of my back pocket. "Where do we get limes?"

Yeah, she was officially into my fruit map. "Green dots. If we take Fourth back to my place, there are two trees on the way." I drew my finger across the map and showed her where my place was.

"Let's go."

The lime trees proved much easier than the avocado. We passed on the first because the limes were too pale and the tree had thorns. I knew there was a difference between trees with and without thorns. But I didn't know fancy shit like which breed was better. I did know it was a hell of a lot easier to pick limes when there were no thorns. Especially if you have to climb for them.

The second tree was in front of a restaurant. It was just dark enough that the patrons didn't stare when we picked a few limes. We took enough for a week or so, then we started walking.

"So, uh, have you eaten? Dinner, I mean?" I asked.

She started laughing. "Thankfully, no. My mom wanted to make me dinner. But she's basically the worst cook ever. You saved me."

"I'm pretty much a hero," I said.

She nodded seriously. "Pretty much."

"You ever been to Miguel's on Fourth?"

"Oh, my God. Best tacos ever."

"It's a block from my place. We could get some tacos. You know, if you want." I shrugged like it wasn't a big deal.

13

But this chick was prettier than me. And I was the prettiest boy I knew. If it took tacos to keep her around for another hour, then I was so buying tacos.

"Depends." She snagged the map out of my back pocket again. She definitely copped a feel. "What are the chances you've got radishes on this thing?"

I laughed. "Not good. Roots are way harder to pin down. But I can do you one better."

"How so?"

"I've got radishes in my garden."

"Of course you have a garden."

"Well, yeah. But it's mostly an excuse to play in the dirt."

"Obviously."

"Obviously. So you in for Miguel's?" I asked.

"Totally."

Miguel's wasn't exactly a sit-down place. They had one table and a short counter. There were always two cooks working. I was amazed at their ability to function in a kitchen that was about ten feet across. But those guys made badass tacos. We left with a bag and headed to my apartment. It wasn't much, but I had my very own little back yard, which was the entire reason I had rented the place.

I mixed some guac while she sliced radishes. It was nice, I suppose. She kept flipping her hair out of her eyes while she was cutting. It just kept falling back. For some reason I found that super sexy.

We spread our loot on the table in my garden. I found the table two summers ago in an alley and dragged it home. I spent the rest of that summer sanding and re-sanding, then priming and painting, and more painting and sealing until I had my very own teal and orange table. She complimented the colors, which was a win.

It was pretty dark out back. Well, as dark as it ever got in a city. So I lit the big candles around my garden. She grinned at me in the flickering light. A couple years back, I had picked up some solar outdoor lights, but they kept breaking. I figured that candles had worked for centuries, and they didn't need a warranty. If she thought it was nice, then that was a bonus.

"You were right," she said.

"About what?"

"You do make awesome guac."

I grinned. "I told you." I opened a couple foil-wrapped tacos and handed her one.

"Thanks." She pulled on her beer, then dug into the taco. "So what else is on that map?"

I worked it out of my pocket again and tossed it on the table. "It's pretty basic. I'm still working on it. There's a lot that grows in SoCal."

She studied the map. "What are the purple dots?"

"Blackberry. But I think there's only one blackberry bush. The pink is pomegranate."

"Blue is avocado." She pointed. "And green is lime. I take it yellow is lemon."

"You're totally smart."

"I know. What about black? And red?"

"Black is apricot. Red is banana. And plantain, but there's only one plantain and it's next to a banana, so." I shrugged.

"Where are the peaches?"

"Teal." I pointed out the various peach trees. "There are figs everywhere. That's the dark purple. But you don't like figs."

"Not even a little bit. My grandmother was obsessed. Whenever we visited her when I was a kid, she would force me to eat them. It compounded the whole hating them thing."

"Valid."

"What else is there?" she asked.

"Persimmon, guava, plum." I tapped various points. "A buddy of mine said there's a papaya tree up here." I pointed to the northern section of the map. "But I haven't found it yet."

"How the hell is all this growing in an urban area?"

I shrugged. "Weather is good for it. City is old. Plus, we're in a port city. Lots of people from lots of places."

"Aww, that's kinda sweet." She smiled. "Diversity in fruit."

I decided I liked it when she smiled. A lot.

"Okay, what about this one?" she asked. "It's kinda lime green."

"That's the best. Kumquats."

"There aren't kumquats here," she said.

"I swear. It's damn near impossible to get to them. The tree is huge. But it's in a park so, technically, it's fair game. I usually end up climbing it at, like, midnight. Fewer people yell at me then."

"What makes it fair game?"

"Public property. As long as it's growing on public property, it's public. Same goes if it's invading public property. So if it's growing in someone's backyard, but the branches are over the sidewalk or an alleyway or whatever, then it's public," I said.

"How did you learn all this crap?"

"It's weird, actually. There's this art collective that publishes fruit maps. Fallen Fruit or something. It's cool, I guess. When I was in school, a girl dragged me to some lecture they gave. I slept through most of it, but I got the gist."

"So overhanging public property?"

"Yeah."

"Okay, then I think we can do it."

"Do what?" I asked.

"Get you an orange."

"Seriously? How?"

"Marion is out of town until tomorrow evening. She has a dickwad neighbor who watches her place, but he's in his eighties. He's probably asleep now. He'll wake up in an hour or so, flip on his outdoor lights all angry and shit, then go back to bed. He does the same thing every two or three hours," she said.

"Shut the fuck up. How do we get an orange?"

"Same way we got the avocados."

"I'm so in." I polished off my last taco and grabbed a handful of radish slices. "How long do we wait?"

She shrugged. "Finish the guac. Start walking. We can sit on my mom's porch and wait until he hits the lights. About fifteen minutes after that and we're good to go."

"This is awesome."

"How long have you been casing the joint?" she asked.

I thought about that. I'd watched the tree last year, but I'd given up pretty quickly. The current obsession had been for the last few weeks. "Three weeks, maybe." That made me sound crazy. "At first I would just walk by every couple days, then a couple times a day. I only started standing there and watching a couple days ago."

"Not nearly as stalkerish as I thought."

"Not at all stalkerish. But I'm sorry if I freaked your mom out," I said.

"You didn't. She only noticed you tonight, so you were pretty stealthy."

"Good to know. I guess. Although, ability to stalk without being detected is probably not a good trait."

"You can't really put it on a résumé," she said.

"And if you can, I don't think I want that job."

"Agreed."

"You want to get out of here?" I asked.

She nodded. We did a quick cleanup. I grabbed my sweatshirt and we headed out.

We took a different route back so I could show her a couple more trees. Each one seemed more exciting to her, which was awesome. Mostly because I was the only chick I knew who got excited about fruit trees.

When we got to the house, she left me on the porch to go check on her mom. She came back a couple minutes later and handed me a cold, fresh beer.

"We're out of limes. But I figured you'd have that covered."

I laughed and dug into my bag. "Here." I gave her a handful or limes and a couple bananas. "Leave 'em in a bowl on the table for your mom. My mom loves crap like that."

She arched an eyebrow. "Thoughtful, too. You win today."

"I win every day."

She laughed and went back in the house. When she came out, she handed me a wedge of lime. I twisted it into my bottle. As she sat down, the lights turned on across the street.

"See? I told you," she whispered.

"How long does he leave them on for?" I whispered back.

"Five minutes or so. Just long enough to scowl at the neighborhood."

She was right. Two minutes later, an ancient guy in a fluffy robe came out to stand on his porch. He squinted at us and glared at a couple shadows. Then he shuffled to the other side of his deck, squinted at someone else, glared at some other shadow, and went back inside. A minute later, the lights went out. I didn't realize how bright they were until they were gone.

"Christ, what's with the industrial strength security lights?"

"No clue. He's old and crazy. Isn't that enough of a reason for over-the-top security lights?"

"Good point. But I may have gone blind."

"Probably. That's tragic."

"Oh, well. Sight is overrated. I have four other senses that function perfectly."

She laughed. "Good."

And then she leaned over and kissed me. I was right. Sight was unnecessary. Her lips were smooth and cool. I tasted the tang of fresh lime and the headiness of beer. She traced my jaw with her fingertips. Briefly tasted my bottom lip. Kissed me one last time, then leaned back.

"Want to go get an orange now?"

"Umm." I suddenly didn't care much about the orange. "Yes. Orange."

"Come on." She stood and held out her hand. I took it. We left our beers on the porch railing and crossed the street.

"There's a good one up on that weird curvy branch." I pointed.

"Where? Oh, yeah. I see it. Ready?"

I cupped my hands so she could hop up. Once again, she braced herself on my shoulder and jumped. After a minute of rustling and a frustrated sigh, she shout-whispered, "I got it."

"Okay, I'm going to drop you."

She landed next to me and held out a massive orange. "Now what?"

I pulled out my pocket knife and sliced into the rind. I dug the blade in until it reached the center. After making a second and third cut, I was able to wrestle out two fat pieces. I offered one to her. We grinned at each other and bit in. It was sweet and tart. Juice dripped down my fingers.

Best orange ever.

RECIPE FOR LIBERATED ORANGE SLICES

Directions

1. Find an orange tree on public property (if you can't reach it from the sidewalk, it's not public).

2. Pick an orange.

3. Slice rind.

4. Peel rind.

5. Split into sections.

6. Eat.

THE LUSCIOUS *TARTE AUX FRAISES*

HISTORIA

MARIE FRANCOISE LET HER HEAD hang down for a few seconds to rest her neck muscles. But this hurt her throat, and she felt like she was choking. So she lifted her head again, holding it high. She heard the "clock, clock" of a woman's footsteps. Someone was coming. She quickly turned her eyes toward the sound of the footsteps to see who it was. Ugh. Mme. Lecourier, that nasty old biddy, was approaching the square. Marie Francoise quickly turned her eyes away and stared stonily in front of her.

Because the pillory was about five feet above ground level, she could see, in the distance, the *place* where the beautiful gypsy girl had been hanged a few days before. She fixed her gaze resolutely on the spot where the young girl had lost her life, and so didn't have to see the lady's eyes as she peered up at her, judging her. Still, she couldn't help but hear her "tsk," and her "stupid girl" as she passed the pillory.

She thought about her friend Jeannette for a few moments. She had stolen the *tarte aux fraises* for Jeannette. She had seen it in the window of the shop, along with all the other freshly baked and fragrant pies and cakes. She had noticed the plump, red, glistening strawberries, and had thought, "Jeannette's favorite." Before she had a chance to talk herself out of it, she had taken it. She had run to Jeannette's house with the pie, and Jeannette had been very happy to see her, and the pie.

Jeannette had put her infant daughter down for a nap, and then while talking, mainly about the hanging, they had eaten the pie together. The luscious treat. After that, Jeannette had warmly embraced Marie Francoise, saying, "How thoughtful of you to bring me a treat when I'm stuck here all day with the baby. How nice you are to me, my friend."

Marie Francoise felt a warmth now, beginning in her loins and radiating through her entire body, when she thought of that hug and the look in Jeannette's eyes. She hung onto the thought of Jeannette saying, "How nice you are to me" while looking into her eyes.

Jeannette always looked right into her eyes and Marie Francoise was sure that she saw her feelings for Jeannette— how badly she wanted to kiss Jeannette, and wished that they could be alone together. Jeannette seemed to welcome those thoughts. Was it possible that Jeannette felt the same?

Marie Francoise loved how Jeannette never criticized her for being a bad wife, for neglecting her duties. The other young wives laughed at her, sometimes behind her back and sometimes not, saying that she acted like a child instead of a grown woman. Marie Francoise's aunt, who had raised her like a mother, called her a shirker because, instead of cooking and cleaning for her husband, Robert, as she should, she was often caught just sitting and daydreaming.

She thought of Jeannette's mouth, with its full red lips, and how it formed into a little smile when she talked to her.

"Jeannette, Jeannette," she thought. "How I wish you were here with me. How I wish I could see you."

They had both been shocked and sad about the gypsy girl's hanging. Marie Francoise didn't believe the gypsy girl had done what they said she had done, but thought her only crime was being a beautiful girl with creamy skin, who could dance and who had a clever pet goat. And who didn't quite have the proper clothing. She had harmed no one. Jeannette agreed with Marie Francoise about all of this.

The world around her was mad, she thought. When anything was too pretty or too enjoyable, people felt they had to destroy it.

"Stop thinking about the hanged gypsy girl," she told herself. She turned her thoughts back to Jeannette, and again felt the warm vibration that began at her center and radiated through her whole body. She liked that feeling, and didn't believe it made her bad. Why would such a thing exist, and be so readily there, if it was a sin? It was no worse than hunger for food, or an itch that needed scratching, or a baby who needed to be held. The priests had to be wrong, it just didn't make sense that the feeling was sinful.

What she felt for Jeannette had its own character. It was like warm buzzing that sometimes became a throbbing vibration—a vibration that took on a life of its own, and couldn't be ignored. She wished she could touch herself now, to bring that throb to a climax. But her hands were locked in place by the pillory's mechanism until sundown. She sighed, thinking that it wasn't even close to noon. It was June, so sundown wouldn't come for more than eight hours. She strained against her prison again, trying to move it or loosen it, even though she knew it was useless.

A strange thing happened when she pushed against the restraining wooden mechanism the second time. The mild buzzing that she had been feeling when she was thinking of Jeannette suddenly turned into a roaring, throbbing vibration. The pleasure was so intense that she let out a small cry. Marie Francoise looked quickly about, but there was no one near. Soon there would be more people, as the noon hour approached, but right now there was a lull in the human and animal traffic through the center of the town. The women were home, preparing the midday meal, and the men were about their work. Clerics, students, notaries— everyone was working. Soon there would be more people passing by on their way home to eat. Her own husband, a junior woodworker, would be at the cathedral with his master and the apprentice until evening. The monks would feed them their midday meal.

She strained against the stocks again, liking the feeling that came to her, a much more powerful feeling than anything she had ever felt while touching herself or imagining that she was kissing or touching Jeannette. Again she cried out involuntarily. She squeezed her legs together to try to get some relief from that aching, throbbing vibration.

She strained against the wooden apparatus again, knowing it would make her cry out and that she would be unable to stop herself. The feeling was even stronger this time, roaring through her body. She let out a scream, and then quickly looked around to see if anyone had heard. No one. She squeezed the muscles of her loins together, trying to make herself have an orgasm. Again, she pushed against the wood, as if trying to free herself, a moan escaping her. She squeezed her muscles together. She did these two things over and over, each time screaming or moaning, and each time thinking she couldn't bear the force of the feeling. She came, screaming again, and the spasms wracking her body with unbelievable pleasure. It seemed like the orgasm lasted a minute or more.

When it began to subside, she wished she could lie down and rest, but, of course, she was stuck in the apparatus until sundown.

She suddenly began to worry that Robert, a serious and somewhat stern young man, would hear about her being put on the pillory while he was at work at the cathedral. She knew he would have to hear about it eventually, because the many wagging tongues of Paris's women—and men—made that inevitable. But she hoped he wouldn't hear until tonight, on his way home, by which time she'd be released.

She wasn't worried that he would be angry. That was a foregone conclusion. He constantly lectured her for her childish ways, her forgetfulness, her daydreaming. She was as playful as he was serious. When they had first met, it was her pretty, laughing face and playful ways that had drawn him. But now that they had been married for two years, it seemed that her playfulness, her childishness, no longer suited him. It seemed that he wanted her to be just like him, an old person in a young person's body! He often said to her, "What will happen when a child comes? Will you be able to take care of him?"

No, she knew he would be angry, but she worried that he would also be ashamed of her. Of how she was stuck up here all day like an animal in a cage, while people walked by and taunted her, or threw things at her.

His own wife, an object of ridicule! How would he be able to stand it?

Some children had thrown apples at her this morning, and it could get worse than that—people often threw eggs, cabbages, rotten fruit, or even bricks or stones at those stuck on the pillory. Would Robert, on hearing what had happened, leave the cathedral and walk over here to see her? She hoped not. How long would it be, she wondered, before he forgave her?

Her theft of the pie had been discovered only this morning. Someone—she didn't know who—had seen her take it from the shop. That person had then told the shop owner, and the shop owner had told one of the king's guards. So they had come to her home (really, the home of Robert's parents), and taken her to the pillory. She had gone with them quietly, knowing there was no escape, and that denying it would do no good. The king's guards were known for not listening, and for roughing people up for fun. By the time they had come, her husband had already left the house. The work the woodworker and his helpers were doing at the cathedral was very important, and work started early and ended late. Every door in the public part of the church was being replaced, and more than thirty doors had to be carved, and then installed. Needless to say, the work had to be perfect.

So, although she knew it was inevitable that Robert would find out about her being pilloried, she hoped that it would be later, rather than sooner.

Again, she heard a woman's steps, and wondered who was coming. This time, she didn't want to look to see who it was. She decided to keep staring fixedly ahead, and ignore the person. It was probably her Aunt Elizabeth, come to berate her.

The steps drew closer and closer, and whoever it was (a person her own age, she could tell, and not her aunt) stopped directly in front of the pillory and stood looking up at her.

"Marie Francoise."

"Jeannette!" said Marie Francoise. It came out as a squeak because she hadn't spoken all day. The only sounds she had made since the morning were her moans of pleasure. Thinking of this, she blushed. Then she smiled at Jeannette, and said, "You came to see me! Who's watching Anne-Lise?"

Jeannette stared at Marie Francoise with a stricken look on her face. "Your poor neck! How can they do this to *you*?"

"I'm all right," said Marie Francoise. "It's not so bad."

"I didn't know you had stolen that pie. And for me! I feel terrible, thinking of how much I enjoyed it. Why did you steal it?"

"The idea just took hold of me, to take it, and I did. I can't explain it." She tried to recreate the moment in her mind so as to explain it to Jeannette. "I just don't know why. I could have asked Robert for the money, or taken it out of the money he gives me for food. Or I could even have baked a pie myself, though I'm not very good at that. But I didn't do any of those things. I just took it, knowing it was your favorite." She stole a glance at Jeannette to see whether she felt any pleasure from Marie Francoise knowing that strawberry pie was her favorite, and saw the little smile. Then she asked again, "But where's the baby?"

"My mother has her. I heard what happened, and I had to come. Marie Francoise, it was sweet of you to think of me, but please don't ever steal for me again." Her always-smiling mouth wasn't smiling, and she looked as stern as Marie Francoise had ever seen her look.

Marie Francoise couldn't stand any more criticism, judgment, or sternness—especially not from Jeannette—and she felt her mouth turning down. She was going to cry, and there was no way of stopping it. She knew that tears would soon be falling down on the paving stones way below her. And that is exactly what happened. Big plops of tears fell right in front of Jeannette's feet.

"Stop, now, my dear friend. I'm sorry I said that," said Jeannette. "I can't stand for you to cry. Please, please…steal for me whenever you like!"

This made both of them laugh. Then Marie Francoise said, "You're right. It was stupid. I won't do it again. Robert is right about me. I'm nothing but a silly girl. The guards could have hurt me, or some rowdy student might break my head with a brick later today. What I did was dangerous, and stupid. But…"

"What?"

"I felt so happy when I saw that you really enjoyed it, and when you told me how nice I was, and when—when you hugged me."

At this Jeannette said nothing, but looked up at Marie Francoise, looked directly into her eyes. The look seemed to penetrate right into Marie Francoise's body. First into her heart, filling it with warmth, and making it suddenly matter very little that she was being humiliated in front of the entire city. Then into her belly, which did a few flip-flops. Then into her loins, where the heat began to grow again. The two young women stared into each other's eyes for a long while. Then Jeannette said, "Marie Francoise?"

"What?" the other answered dreamily.

"Please come to my house tomorrow, while your husband is at work."

"I would like that," said Marie Francoise.

"And don't steal me a pie, because I'm going to bake a pie tomorrow. Not a strawberry pie, but an apple pie this time, with black walnuts. Would you like that?"

"Of course!" said Marie Francoise. "I'll come over in the morning."

But Marie Francoise remembered how angry her husband was going to be, and said, "Robert might lock me up, or something, because I've been pilloried. I may not be able to come over."

"That's all right. Then we'll just wait until he's over it."

Or I might be able to sneak out, thought Marie Francoise.

"It'll be fun, Marie Francoise," continued Jeannette. "We'll talk, and we'll play with the baby, and we'll eat a piece of pie. And you'll tell me all about what happens the rest of today, all right?"

"Yes, that will be nice." Marie Francoise thought the time would fly by, now that she had something to look forward to tomorrow. Even if the worst happened, and Robert came to look at her while she was up on the pillory, she could tell Jeannette about it tomorrow...or whenever she was allowed out. And even if someone hurled a brick at her, it wouldn't be so bad if she could tell her friend about it.

Marie Francoise said, "You'd better get back. It'll be time to feed Anne-Lise." She looked at Jeannette's plump breasts contained in the tight bodice, and wished she could touch them. Then, in her mind's eye, she saw herself suckling at Jeannette's right breast, and fondling the other with her right hand. She also imagined looking up at Jeannette's face while she was doing this, and seeing her grow more and more excited. She realized that she was still staring down at Jeannette's breasts, and turned very red. Her face felt hot, and she thought it must be the color of a strawberry.

She raised her eyes to Jeannette's face abashedly, and saw, to her amazement, that Jeannette was smiling broadly and knowingly, as if she knew what Marie Francoise was thinking…and as if she liked it.

TARTE AUX FRAISES (STRAWBERRY PIE)

Ingredients

2 (9-inch) unbaked pie crusts (homemade or store-bought)

4 cups fresh strawberries, halved

3/4 cup granulated sugar

1/3 cup all-purpose flour

2 tablespoons butter, cut into little pieces

1 egg, well beaten

Directions

1. Preheat oven to 425 degrees F. Bake 1 crust for 10 minutes. Remove from oven and let cool.

2. Place strawberries in a bowl; gently mix together with sugar and flour. Pour strawberries into cooled crust, and dot fruit with butter or margarine. Lay other unbaked crust over it and seal the edges. Poke holes around top with a fork. Brush with egg.

3. Bake 35 to 45 minutes, or until crust is slightly browned.

WHINING AND DINING

JAE

I was close to whining as I called my best friend. The phone rang, and I glared at the stove while I waited for Remy to pick up, determined not to be bested by a pot of pasta. If you could call the limp mess in the pot pasta.

Good thing my *nonna* couldn't see me now. Since the beginning of time, every Sorrentino had been a chef. My parents, all three of my siblings, and more aunts, uncles, and cousins than I could count were in the food business. When I, the *bambina* of the family, had been born, nature had apparently decided that it was time for some genetic variety, and as a result, I couldn't cook to save my life. God knows I had tried, but after I'd nearly burned down the family restaurant at the age of twelve, I'd been banned from the kitchen.

Well, at least I was a champ at taste-testing. And I had a best friend who could perform magical feats with the meager contents of my fridge.

"This is a culinary emergency," I said as soon as Remy picked up the phone. "I need help with this damn chicken."

"Is it attacking you?"

I could practically hear the smile in her voice. "Very funny. Can you come over? I need cooking lessons."

"Cooking lessons?" Remy echoed. "Is hell freezing over?"

Well, at least she wasn't laughing. I had to give her credit for that. And she was right—whenever she had offered cooking lessons, I had declined, but now I had the right motivation. "I tried on my own, but…well…"

"What did you make?" Remy asked in a how-bad-is-it tone.

"Rubbery chicken breast, too salty sauce, and overcooked pasta."

"I take it that wasn't what you were aiming for?"

I flicked an overly limp noodle into the sink. "Would you stop teasing and just come over to save my cooking-challenged butt?"

"Why me? Why not ask your brothers or your sister or—?"

"And have them make fun of me for the next fifty years? No, thanks." Besides, I hadn't seen Remy for a while, and I missed spending time with her. "Will you help me, please?"

"I'm on my way," Remy said and hung up.

With the phone still pressed to my ear, I stood there for a moment before I kicked myself into motion. My knight in a not-so-shiny chef jacket was on her way, so I'd better make the most incriminating evidence of my cooking disaster disappear before she arrived.

"Okay." Remy surveyed the battlefield that was my kitchen. "What's going on here? Why are you cooking?"

From the moment she'd first started working in my parents' restaurant five years ago, Remy and I had been best buds who could tell each other everything. She knew all about my romantic exploits, so I saw no reason to lie to her.

"This is just a test run, but I have to figure out how to wine and dine a woman by Saturday."

Remy set down her knife roll on the granite countertop, glanced at the ruins of my cooking experiment, and arched an eyebrow.

I rubbed my neck. "Well, I admit the dining part isn't going so well, but I'm not giving up."

"Who would have thought," Remy murmured. "Lucia Sorrentino spending the day slaving away over the stove—voluntarily."

I shrugged. "The things we do for love..."

"Yeah." Remy sighed softly.

I tilted my head and studied her. As usual, her blond hair was tied back in a ponytail, but a few stubborn strands refused to be tamed, and she repeatedly pushed them out of her blue eyes. She looked like she always did, but something seemed off. "You okay? I didn't interrupt anything when I called, did I?"

"No. You know me. There's nothing to interrupt."

"You should go out more. Date." She hadn't dated anyone since breaking up with that creep Barbara two years ago.

Remy shook her head, making more blond tendrils fall onto her face. She shoved them away. "I work for your slave-driving parents. I don't have time to date."

"Bullshit. You're just too chicken to put your heart on the line again."

She looked at me for a moment, a strange expression on her face, and then shrugged. "You do know that insulting someone who wields very big, very sharp knives for a living is a bad idea, don't you?"

Especially if that someone could debone a chicken in ten seconds flat, even with her eyes closed and one hand tied behind her back. Good thing I wasn't a chicken. "And you know that changing the subject won't do you any good with me, don't you?"

"Who's changing the subject? We were discussing your love life, not mine. Why are you trying to woo some poor, unsuspecting woman with your nonexistent cooking skills?"

"We were talking about cooking, and I might have kinda implied that I could make her a romantic dinner that'll blow her socks off."

Again, Remy just arched an eyebrow.

"Well, you know what my *nonna* always said. The way to a woman's heart is through her stomach."

"Yeah. But she also said: Never trust a skinny cook—and you are skinny." She pinched my hip as if proving my lack of padding.

"Hey." I slapped her hand away. "I'm not."

"You are. At least compared to me."

Not that ancient argument again. I rolled my eyes. "So you're carrying a few extra pounds. Big deal. You're still an attractive woman."

Instead of the expected denials, only silence came from Remy.

What was it with her today? "Remy? You with me?"

"Uh, yeah." She shook herself as if trying to clear her head. "So let's sum this up. You promised to dazzle your latest flavor of the month with a romantic dinner. You couldn't impress her with some other impossible task instead? Like bringing down the moon for her—or merely buying her flowers."

"She doesn't like flowers."

Remy snorted. "Every woman likes flowers."

"You don't."

"I'm a chef. I like my greenery on a plate."

"So is she."

Remy stared at me as if I'd said my prospective girlfriend was a three-headed T. rex. "You're dating a chef? But you always said that you'd never want to date someone in the food business after growing up with a horde of chefs."

Was it just my imagination, or did she sound almost hurt? "I'm not dating her. Not yet. But I'm sure a woman like Alexandra Beaumont won't be able to resist my romantic dinner." That was, if she didn't succumb to food poisoning first.

Remy's eyes widened. "Alexandra Beaumont? *The* Alexandra Beaumont, celebrity chef with a national cooking show, her own line of cooking gear, and half a dozen cookbooks?"

Grinning, I buffed my nails on my shirt. "Yep. That's her."

"Jesus." Remy sank against the kitchen counter. "How did you meet?"

"I'm doing the promo for her new book. Something about braising, whatever that is."

Remy covered her face with her hands for a moment. "You don't know what braising is, but you want to cook her dinner? Are you sure you don't want to use the good old flower method?"

I gave her *the* look. Over the years, I had perfected it watching *Nonna* and my parents stare down the new line cooks. It never failed to work with any chef, and Remy wasn't an exception.

"Okay, okay." She held up her hands. "Who am I to throw stones? It's not like I'm a champ in the making-healthy-decisions department when it comes to my love life, either."

"So you'll help me?"

Now it was Remy's turn to give me *the* look. "Is dessert the best part of a meal? Of course I will. Sadly, I think my famous spinach soufflé with angel hair pasta and white chocolate crème brûlée for dessert is out of the question, considering your usual method of cooking is removing the tin foil and nuking."

I caressed the microwave, my most trusted kitchen utensil. "Hey, don't knock it till you've tried it."

Remy grimaced. "No, thanks. So let's see…" She checked my fridge. "You can do macaroni and cheese, right?"

"Of course." On a good day, at least.

"Good. Then we'll do that."

"Uh, I don't think that will impress Alexandra."

Remy patted my hand. "Don't worry. My version will. We're making zucchini pasta alla panna." Familiar with where I kept things in my kitchen, she opened one of the cupboards and took out my kiss-the-cook apron. When she turned toward the counter and tied the apron strings around her waist, I couldn't help noticing what a fine behind she had.

Overweight, my ass. Or rather, her ass. I tore my gaze away. Christ, what was wrong with me? I hadn't ogled her ass—or any other of her body parts—for a long time. When I first met her, I'd felt an instant spark of attraction, but we'd both been in relationships back then, and as time went by, I'd learned to see her as Remy, the most loyal friend in the world, not a potential *flavor of the month*, as Remy called my usually short-lived relationships.

I didn't want to ruin the best friendship I'd ever had, so I had to remind myself that Remy wasn't on the menu today. Or on any other day, for that matter.

She took the lone zucchini that led a miserable existence in my refrigerator and washed it. With a flick of her wrist, she unrolled her knife kit and pulled out one of the knives.

The familiar rat-a-tat-tat echoed through my kitchen as Remy made fast work of the zucchini, slicing it into thin ribbons, each piece exactly the same size. Her hands moved like those of a pianist, not one wrong move.

Poetry in motion.

I found myself unable to look away from her hands. They were a chef's hands, strong and nimble and covered in a familiar pattern of scars, burn marks, and calluses.

As if she could sense my gaze on her, Remy stopped slicing and dicing and turned toward me. "Something wrong?"

"Uh…" I wrenched my gaze away from her hands and blindly pointed at a red welt running across one of her knuckles. "What happened there?"

Remy rubbed her knuckle. "A little run-in with a cheese grater who had it in for me." She went back to cutting the zucchini, and I went back to watching her hands.

"You should really have your own cooking show too."

"Nah," Remy said without looking up. "I belong in the kitchen, not in front of a camera. Besides, I didn't even go to culinary school."

"You learned from *Nonna* and my parents. That beats culinary school."

Remy chuckled. "I call it the School of Hard Knocks." She glanced over her shoulder at me. "I thought you wanted to learn and not just watch. Come on, you can be my sous chef."

I took the mallet she handed me and pounded the two chicken breasts she had pulled from the fridge, taking out my sexual frustration on the poor fowl. Yeah, sexual frustration. That had to be why I couldn't keep my eyes off my best friend today. It had merely been too long. That was all.

Bam! Bam! Bam!

I was just beginning to enjoy cooking when Remy grabbed my arm. "No need to kill it. It's already dead."

Her touch made my arm tingle. What the fuck? Quickly, I pulled away and busied myself with seasoning the chicken.

"Careful on the salt." Remy stopped me with a touch to my hand, causing another tingle to shoot down to my toes—and all the places in between.

Christ. I had to clear my throat twice before I could speak. "What now?"

"Now you sauté the chicken breasts." Remy handed me a pan.

Remembering something about chicken having to be well cooked for safety reasons, I cranked the heat on the stove up as far as it would go, poured in a bit of olive oil, and turned to the sink, glad that I could turn my back to Remy while washing my hands. What I really needed was a cold shower. My skin felt overheated from a simple touch between friends. How could that be? I let the water run for a minute, hoping to wash off the feeling.

No such luck.

When I turned back around, Remy was mincing garlic. Wisps of hair had escaped her ponytail and curled charmingly at her neck and cheeks that were flushed with the heat from the stove.

Heat? Shit! I remembered the pan and hurried back to the stove.

The oil in the pan hissed and spat at me like an angry cat, challenging me.

I took a step back and craned my neck to peer into the pan from a safe distance.

Smoky steam curled up.

"Uh, Remy."

When she turned around, her eyes widened. She jumped toward the stove and reached out to put a lid on the pan.

With a flash, the overheated oil burst into flame.

Remy dropped the lid on the pan and reared back, clutching her face.

My blood ran cold despite the heat in the kitchen. "Remy! Remy, are you okay?" *Please, please, please, be okay.* I rushed over, nearly stumbling over my own feet in my haste to get to Remy, and gently pried her hands off her face.

"I'm fine." She peered up at me from under singed bangs. Red dots marred her cheeks.

With trembling hands, I reached out and trailed one finger across her cheekbone. "Oh, God, Remy. I—"

Her eyes fluttered shut. She swayed softly.

Or was I the one swaying? I wasn't sure. "Are you really okay?" I took her face between both of my hands, careful not to press too hard on the tiny burn marks.

She opened her eyes. Emotions swirled through the blue depths too fast for me to identify. "I'm fine," she said, her voice hoarse.

Behind her, smoke from the smothered fire filled the kitchen, but I couldn't care less. All I could think of was Remy, safe in my arms. For a moment, I nearly pulled her close and kissed her, giddy with relief. I stopped myself before I could actually do it. I'd made enough of a mess already. "I'm so, so sorry," I said, not sure what I was apologizing for—nearly blowing her up or nearly blowing her mind by kissing her.

If she would have thought it mind-blowing, which was doubtful. Just because we were both gay didn't mean we were attracted to each other.

I repeated it to myself a few times. Nope, no attraction there, just friendship.

"Don't worry." Remy ran a hand through her bangs and smiled crookedly. "I needed a haircut."

We looked at each other and burst out laughing, the strange tension between us gone.

At least for the moment.

Finally, I let go of her and went to open the window while Remy checked on the blackened pan. I needed some fresh air.

I was back to watching Remy instead of helping with the cooking. With a glance up at the black stain on the ceiling above the stove, I told myself it was safer that way. But as I admired the way Remy tossed the zucchini in the pan with a practiced flip of her wrist, it felt anything but safe.

She added a generous amount of cream and let it simmer for a few minutes before seasoning it with basil and lemon juice. As she stirred the mix, her hips swayed softly. Her nose wriggled like that of the animated rat from the Disney movie that had earned her the nickname Remy.

Clouds of steam and the aroma of garlic and fresh herbs rose from the pan, making my mouth water. I leaned closer to breathe in the enticing smell—and realized I was inhaling the scent of Remy's perfume, not that of the pasta alla something.

Jesus. I clutched the counter next to me, feeling light-headed. Had to be low blood pressure, right?

That hypothesis bit the dust as Remy dipped a spoon into the pan, raised it to her mouth, and slowly slid it between her full lips. Her tongue flicked out and licked a bit of sauce from the corner of her mouth.

Heat shot through me, and it had nothing to do with the temperature in my tiny kitchen.

Remy hummed and reached for the cream. "Good. Might be a bit too hot, though."

I tore at the collar of my shirt. Yes, it was hot for sure.

After stirring in a bit more cream, she tried the sauce again and let out a moan that made my body tingle in a way it never had around her before. She took a new spoon, dipped it into the pan, and held it out toward me. "Taste this."

I hesitated as if she were holding out an apple from the Garden of Eden, but something in her eyes beckoned me forward. Slowly, I shuffled closer.

Remy held still, barely even breathing, except that her hand with the spoon was trembling a bit. Her eyes darkened to azure.

From just inches away, I could see the tiny red marks dotting her flushed face. Why did it suddenly feel so natural to want to kiss them all better?

Without looking away from Remy, I leaned forward, drawn in by her scent and her heat. My gaze darted from the burn marks to her lips.

They were moving. Whispering something. My name.

Lured by that siren call, I leaned in.

Something between us stopped my forward movement.

I blinked down at the forgotten spoon Remy still held. Afraid to glance up and see a look of confusion—or, worse, dismay—on her face, I bent and closed my lips around the spoon.

A harmony of flavors exploded on my tongue, making my taste buds dance a tango. I moaned and barely resisted the urge to lick the spoon—or Remy's neck. "It's…" I cleared my throat. "Delicious." Slowly, I glanced up.

The look in her darkened eyes made something inside of me burst into flames.

I surged forward, pinned her against the center island, and kissed her.

The spoon clattered to the floor as her hands came up and threaded in my hair, pulling me closer. She nipped my bottom lip and teased the corner of my mouth with her tongue.

Not that I needed much convincing to open my mouth to her.

Our tongues slid hotly against each other as we tumbled against the counter.

It took a few moments for me to realize that the ringing in my ears had nothing to do with the effect her kiss had on me. Groaning, I pulled back and hurled a glare at the egg timer that Remy had set for the pasta before turning back to her.

We stared at each other.

"Oh, wow. It's… You… I…" Great. Here I was, one of LA's most sought-after book publicists, reduced to helpless stammering by a mere kiss. All right. Maybe it had been much more than just a mere kiss. I touched my lips, seared by her passion. "What the hell was in that sauce?"

A tiny smile quirked Remy's lips, then spread over her whole face when I didn't pull out of her embrace. She looked into my eyes, swallowed, and said, "Love."

I opened my mouth and then closed it before opening it again. "You…? You mean…?"

Remy nodded, looking just as dazed as I felt. "I fell in love with you the first time I saw you, sneaking into the kitchen to steal some of your grandmother's dessert, but you never noticed me. At least not that way."

No, I sure didn't, at least not after we had become friends. God, how could I have been so blind? I rubbed my good-for-nothing eyes. "Why didn't you ever say something?"

"After you rejected that amorous sous chef, telling her you'd never date someone who works in the food business?" She shook her head. "Our friendship means too much to me to ever risk it on something that is hopeless anyway."

I cupped her red-dotted cheek in my palm. "Looks like it's not so hopeless after all."

"When did you…?"

"Today. I don't know why, but as soon as we started cooking, I suddenly noticed you in a way that I never had before."

We stared at each other, then leaned in simultaneously. Our mouths met, this time much gentler, but not an ounce less passionate.

"It's like your grandmother always said," Remy whispered against my lips between kisses. "Cooking is magic."

I hummed my agreement but didn't answer, too busy kissing her.

Remy pressed her hands against my shoulders and pushed.

I drew back with a groan of protest, hoping like hell that she hadn't changed her mind about me. About us.

"What about Alexandra Beaumont?" she asked, breathing heavily.

"Alexandra who?" I shook my head. Compared to that mix of warm familiarity and brand-new excitement I felt for Remy, my interest in Alexandra seemed lukewarm at best. "It seems I'll have to cancel our dinner plans. I already have a chef in my life after all, and you know what they say about too many cooks spoiling the broth. Plus, I don't think she'd be too impressed with my cooking skills, seeing as this is the second pot of pasta I managed to ruin today." I pointed toward the stove.

Cursing, Remy let go of me and rushed over to the stove to rescue the pasta.

Too late. I had spoiled enough dishes to know when a pot of pasta was beyond hope.

With a crestfallen expression on her face, Remy returned to my embrace. "I never ruined dinner before in my life."

"There's a first time for everything," I murmured and kissed her again. Who knew that her kisses were as addictive as her cooking?

Minutes later, Remy pulled back and glanced at her watch. "I have to go. Both of your parents are still out sick, so I have to open the restaurant tonight."

Nothing like mentioning a girl's parents to cool her ardor. I leaned against the counter and watched Remy take off the apron and roll up her knife case. This time, I let myself admire her ass without qualms. "Let my sister take over tomorrow and come spend the evening with me."

With the knife roll tucked under her arm, she turned and regarded me. "Are you asking me out on a date?"

I nodded. "You still need to teach me how to make dessert, after all." Visions of licking warm chocolate and whipped cream off her skin danced through my head.

The kiss she gave me nearly brought me to my knees. She might have answered my request for dessert-making lessons, but if she did, I didn't hear her over the buzzing in my ears. Then she was gone, leaving me to stare at the black spot on the ceiling.

My kitchen might never be the same again, and neither would I. Grinning, I set out to clean up the mess and tidy the apartment. After all, I had a hot date with a pint of chocolate sauce and my very own domestic goddess tomorrow.

ZUCCHINI PASTA ALLA PANNA

Ingredients
(for two people)

1 zucchini
2 tablespoons olive oil
2 boneless chicken breasts
Salt
Pepper
3 gloves garlic
1 cup cream
Fresh basil
2 tablespoons lemon juice
½ lb. penne pasta, cooked
½ cup grated cheese or parmesan

Directions

1. Slice the zucchini into thin slices lengthwise; then into thin ribbons.

2. Heat olive oil in a frying pan over medium heat.

3. Season the chicken with salt and pepper and sauté them on both sides until cooked through. Cut them into strips and set them aside.

4. Finely mince the garlic and sauté it. Add the zucchini and sauté it. Add the cream and let it simmer for a few minutes. Season it with some fresh basil and freshly squeezed lemon juice.

5. Add the cooked pasta and the cheese and mix.

Buon appetito!

BURN

REBEKAH WEATHERSPOON

I HATE TO SEE YOU cry, but for some reason it takes me so long to come around when I'm the cause of those tears. You've been avoiding me for two days. It's been tough because we live together, but you're good at building those walls around yourself when you need to heal, or when you just need to be the fuck away from me when I've blown it again. You still kiss me goodbye in the morning, though. Mumble something about how I should have a good day. I'm still a little pissed, too, so I mumble the same.

This thing between us started weeks ago. Months ago, really, after your unemployment ran out. We made each other promises. You said you'd find work soon and I said not to worry. I said I had us both covered. But I did worry. I worried about you, I worried about us and when I wasn't trying my hardest not to be selfish, I worried about myself. We have this house and this dog. You were talking to me about adopting a kid, you *still* talk to me about adopting a kid, when the money comes in, and it all starts adding up. We're fine, but I worry. I worry about the future. I worry about us and sometimes I fuck up and I don't know how to communicate this stress to you, so I snap and I pick and

I do it at the worst time ever. These are bad times for me, too, but I seem to know the exact moment when your day is going to shit.

That night I came through the door with a chip on my shoulder. Stupid co-workers, stupider clients, traffic, and then I step in whatever Legend decided he needed to leave right in front of the door. All you did was ask me about my day, but that was enough to put me over, enough to send me on my most recent rant about how clean the house isn't and how I didn't particularly care for lasagna for dinner even though it's my favorite meal.

I'm snapping and hopping around, trying to keep this dog shit from getting all over the place. Forget that it's ruined my sandals and squished up to the side of my foot. When I get out of the shower and after I've taken Legend out for a walk he barely needs since he handled his business on the floor, I come back to the kitchen to find tears streaking down your cheeks. Your arm is under the running faucet.

"What's wrong?" I ask automatically. I'm still annoyed with you and the dog, but I don't like the look on your face.

"Nothing." I can barely hear you, but I can see the angry red way your dark brown skin is puffing up. The burn is kinda big. It looks painful as hell. You wipe your face with the back of your free hand.

I close the still-open oven door and see the lasagna tossed haphazardly on top of the stove. You managed not to drop it at least, I think to myself.

"Do you need to go the hospital?" I ask, still sounding annoyed because I'm a shitty person and I know I'll have to get right back in that traffic to drive you over there. Rush hour lasts forever in this stupid city.

"No," you say. "It'll be fine. You can go ahead and eat."
You slip by me and off to the bathroom where you've stashed
two first aid kits because you bought another one when we
ran out of Band-Aids instead of just buying more Band-Aids.
You're in there a while. I know you're crying when Legend
sits outside the door, whimpering pathetically until you let
him in. I skip the lasagna and head to bed with my laptop.

You come to bed much later, with your arm all bandaged
up. I'm sure you've eaten. You never let the fruits of your
labor go to waste. You don't say a word, but I hear your huffs
and sighs. You can't sit still until Legend hops on the bed and
wedges himself between our legs. He's your security blanket
and in a few minutes you're out cold. I wait awhile, answer
a few more emails, silently curse a few client requests, but
eventually I head back downstairs. You cleaned the whole
kitchen, top to bottom. Cleaned all the dishes, even the big
pot you only use to make lasagna noodles. That pot that you
love to leave in the sink for at least thirty-six hours every
time you use it.

I open the fridge and dig out the lasagna that you've
wrapped perfectly and put away. I slice into it and see that
you've remembered that the meat sauce I really like actually
gives me heartburn that I love to complain about for at
least two days. You've replaced the sausage with chicken and
spinach. I'm skeptical, but I'm starving so I take a huge piece
and pop it in the microwave.

The first bite is heaven. It seems you've changed
everything about it, the meat, the cheese, even the noodles
are more tender. It's light, but satisfying, filling me and
warming me completely, from the inside. I know I shouldn't
have yelled at you.

When I come back to bed, I try to pull you close to say I'm sorry, but you are not having that. Even in your sleep, you are not having it.

The next morning, you're up before me, on the couch with your laptop and your coffee. I say good morning. You nod. I ask what you're doing. You say looking for jobs, but you won't look at me when you say it. I offer to walk Legend. He's under your feet, looking at me, wondering when we're going to make up. He doesn't like choosing between us, but he loves you more. We all know where his loyalty lies. You've already taken him out, you tell me. I ask you how your arm is and that's when you shut down completely. You're tempted to ignore me. I know. I can tell by the way your mouth drops open, by the way your tongue flicks against the back of your teeth. Man, you want to let me have it, but you say your arm is fine. It should be fine in a couple of days.

I know where I'm not wanted so I get my breakfast together, take my coffee to go. I think about leaving without saying goodbye, but that's petty and low. You tell me to have a good day even though I can tell you're fighting the urge to give me the finger.

Two days go by like this. On the third day you're still tense when my alarm goes off. You're up and out of bed again, walking the dog and making the coffee before I even get in the shower. There's usually more in the morning, your lips on my neck, on my chest as I hit the snooze again and again. You say you're going to be home late. You have another interview and then you have to go by your sister's.

I know you need to vent. You need to tell her in private how pissed you are at me and how you sort of want to punch me and you're thinking about moving out. Thank God your sister likes me and she knows I love you. She knows my temper sucks and she'll tell you to tell me things I already know about patience and understanding. She'll tell you to talk to me. Sometimes you do, but this time I think you won't. You don't want to start another fight because you're that close. That might be the tipping point. You might leave for real this time.

Halfway to the office, I call in and tell them I'm working from home. It's not something I like to do, but desperate measures. You're already gone when I get back to the house. Legend is happy to see me. The little asshole. I know there's something I have to do, but first I call your sister.

After I assure her that everything is okay and apologize for calling out of the blue on a Thursday morning, I get my earful.

"Ooo, you're in so much trouble." She teases through the phone. I can hear your youngest nephew fussing in the background.

"I don't know what to do."

"You say you're sorry and then you never do it again. What did you do, anyway?"

"She didn't tell you?"

"No. She texted me an angry face and told me she was coming over, but I didn't get the whole story."

"She made me dinner and I was a complete dick about it. Actually, I've been a dick in general lately. I'm stressed about her not working."

"You think she isn't stressed? She called me crying after her last interview. She didn't even want the job, but she went in for it anyway and the interview was a disaster. The woman told her they had a hair policy and then asked her how attached she was to her dreadlocks. I think you need to lay off her a little."

I immediately feel my stomach drop to my feet. I didn't know about that. I didn't know about any of it. I say so, feeling like the biggest ass ever. "I just wish I could help her."

"You can. She doesn't need you to find a job for her and she doesn't need you to pressure her to look for work. That's all she does. You can find that lady from the last interview, though, and give her a one-two combo to the face. I'm sure that'll help."

"It's a tempting idea, believe me."

"Do something nice for her and then after, just give her a break. She's trying. Imagine if it was the other way around and she was riding your ass."

I know exactly how that would feel, and just how much I would hate it. I've got to fix this.

I thank your sister and promise to do better. She says she's gonna hold me to it. I take a few calls and somewhere in that time, I figure out what I'm going to do. I text your sister one more time, then head to the store and then the mall. I'm back in time for my afternoon video conference. Then I clean, and clean, and clean. How two people generate that much laundry is beyond me. I even tackle that weird smudge under the bathroom mirror that's been bothering me for months. I remember asking you about it and you telling me that you tried everything to get it out. I feel horrible for not believing you.

I text you and tell you not to eat too much over at your sister's. You text back okay, but ask me why. I tell you I want to have dinner with you, together. Your reply is another simple okay, but I know maybe you're not as pissed at me anymore. If you were, you'd tell me you've already eaten, or tell me to go on without you. We've been together a long time.

My plan for the evening is flawless, but the execution not so much. I knew, all along, why you handle the cooking, but sometimes I forget. It's because I'm terrible at it. Frying shouldn't be hard, but it is. Almost, maybe, I nearly burn down the house. Legend is watching me the whole time, fearful of the destruction I'm sure to cause.

Dessert is more of a success. I've made a mess of the kitchen and myself. I clean the kitchen *and* myself up just in time to shower and change before you get home. Your sister helped me out there, too. She promised she'd have you through the door at eight. The look on your face when you walk through the door is everything. I know you found the formal invitation on the welcome mat. The card is in your hand. You're wearing a new dress that I'm sure you picked up for the interview. The aqua blue looks amazing against your dark brown skin, especially in the candlelight. Your locks are up in an elegant bun. You look beautiful.

A curious smile lights up your face. "What's this?"

"An apology."

"For what?" You step closer, with a quiet hello to Legend as he slobbers on your knee. You let me pull you against me. It feels like it's been forever since I last held you. I take your hand and hold your wrist between us. Your arm is still wrapped up.

"It's an apology for this."

"That was my fault. You know I'm clumsy as shit."

"Only when you're upset and that was my fault."

"I'll give you a little credit. You *were* being pretty mean and you did make me cry."

"May I?" I ask. You say it's okay. I pull back the bandage and look at the damaged skin. The burn is worse than I imagined. "Babe," I say, breathing out my horror. "You should have gone to the hospital."

You shrug like it's no big deal. "Meh. It hurts like a bitch, but it'll be fine in a couple of days. Question, though. Not that I mind, but where are your clothes?"

I cover her burn back up as we both look down at the half-apron I'm wearing. I have my boxer briefs on, but besides a smile, that's it. "Is that important?"

"I guess not." You graze my breast with the edge of the card. "What does this invitation to dinner include, exactly?"

"If you'll follow me." I take your hand and lead you around the counter to our makeshift breakfast nook. I remember saying that it was impractical when we moved in, but you made it work.

"I made your favorite." I point to the platter with the crab cakes and rice and kale centered on the table. Your sister was very specific about the kale. I'm very certain I've completely fucked it up.

"I can see that."

"I got the recipe from Opal. There would have been more, but I burned more than half of it."

A look of horror pops up on your face. "You didn't fry these naked, did you?"

I chuckle a bit. "No."

"Okay, good. Scalding oil on this soft skin would be a bad combination." You absently run your fingers down my stomach. You're still looking at the pitiful bounty spread on the tablecloth we've only used once. I'm looking at you. That little scar above your eye you got when you were in high school. You look me in the eye again and I think you know I love you. You put your head on my shoulder.

"So this is the apology, huh?"

"Part of it." I pull the top off another tray, revealing the cupcakes I made. They spell out "IM SORRY" in purple frosting. You laugh this time. "This is another part," I say. "I was wrong. I've been wrong for a while. It shouldn't take your silent treatment to get me to see that."

"Was it just the silent treatment?" You rub your nose against my neck. I'm not sure how much longer and I can just stand there, holding you like this.

"I did talk to your sister," I confess.

"I wish I could get you in line like her."

"Sometimes it takes a fresh set of eyes."

"I'm not hungry right now," you whisper.

"Nah?"

"Uh-uh."

"We can always reheat these later."

"Let's do that." Then you step away from me, back up just a little and start to inch up your skirt. My gaze goes to your smooth legs, but I know where the real show is. I look at your face, see that look I know so well, the look I've been missing these last few days. You want *something*, just not the food.

"Does this mean you forgive me?" I ask. My mouth is dry.

"It means I'm thinking about it." Your hands snake all the way up to your hips. You do this cute little shimmy and work the thong you're wearing down your legs. The slim piece of fabric is left on the floor. I step forward and scoop it up, toss it on top of the shelf before Legend tries to eat it. Your smile is priceless.

"I appreciate the gesture, but it's not the only reason I'm feeling so forgiving."

"Oh yeah?"

You come closer, closer. You take my hand and slip it between your legs. You've gotten yourself all worked up, I think for a moment before I remember that I'm practically naked. I'm sure you enjoy that. Your voice sneaks out in a breathy sigh as I stroke your wet clit. You whisper in my ear. "I got the job."

"That's great!" I say as I pull back just enough to see your face. My hand is still where it belongs. "What's the job?"

See, this is what I get for being a jerk. I didn't even know what position you went in for. You tell me about it. It's something you wanted. It's the pay you wanted and it's not that far from the house. You start on Monday. You haven't been this happy in months. I kiss you 'cause really there's nothing else to do.

"We should really celebrate, shouldn't we," I say.

"Yep." You say.

I think about taking this to the bedroom, but the couch is closer. I scoop you up, your legs around my waist, my hands gripping your ass tight. Down on the cushions you go. I'm on my knees and up your skirt just as the "Yes" leaves your lips. You smell so good, so fresh. You taste so sweet in my mouth. You grip the back of my head, scoring my skin with your nails. The half-inch of hair will hide the welts I hope you leave.

You're begging now. Loud and strained. I'm not making a sound, but in my heart I'm telling you I love you over and over again. And you hear me.

There's more after you come. A second course and then a third. Dessert is you naked on top of me. There's been a break, and intermission if you will, so I can grab my strap and cock, but you finish grinding your hips on top of me, soaking my lap with your cum as you shake and strain, gripping the back of the couch. You collapse on me, your cheek against mine. You'll try some of those crab cakes, you say. And at least three of the cupcakes. You're hungry now, you say. Starved.

SPINACH AND CHICKEN LASAGNA—THE FANCY WAY

Ingredients

(in the order I remember that I need them)

Skinless, boneless chicken breasts

Frozen Spinach

Whole Wheat Lasagna Noodles

Tomato Sauce (however you want to handle that)

Italian Seasoning

Black Pepper

Chopped Garlic

Ricotta Cheese

Shredded Mozzarella Cheese

Shredded Parmesan Cheese

Directions

1. Cook noodles. Set aside.

2. Preheat oven to 375 F.

3. Chop up the chicken. Cook it with black pepper, garlic, and Italian seasonings. Set aside.

4. Thaw spinach. Mix with ricotta, chopped chicken, and parmesan.

5. Grab lasagna pan. Lay down a layer of noodles, followed by a layer of spinach/chicken mixture, and a thin layer of tomato sauce. Repeat until pan is full.

6. Top with mozzarella. Sprinkle Italian seasoning on top to give it that seasoned look.

7. Bake at 375 degrees F until edges are brown and bubbly. Remove and serve immediately if you have no regard for the roof of your mouth.

Makes 1 tray (whatever that means).

ENTRÉES

TOMATO LADY

CHEYENNE BLUE

"Cooeee!"

Sadie placed the final couple of ripe tomatoes into the tray and pressed the button to lower the hoist. Propping the tray onto her hip, she stepped off the platform as it reached the ground. She could see Erica's face peering through the greenhouse door. A flicker of fingers against the plastic as Erica watched her approach.

Sadie stepped outside. It was only 7 a.m. but the morning was already warm and humid. The smell of coffee curled back to her in the sunshine, and she smiled. Her tentative friendship with Erica had recently moved past formality, and Erica had obviously braved the clunky old coffee machine to make a fresh pot before she'd called her.

Erica waited in the open shed where Sadie sold her produce. The older woman was as immaculately turned out as ever, her chestnut hair twisted into a complicated knot on top of her head, her sleeveless blouse wrinkle-free and tucked into an ankle-length skirt. Manicured toes peeped out from leather sandals—sandals that Sadie was sure would cost as much as 15 kilos of her finest baby Roma tomatoes.

"Got time to sit for five?" Erica set down two mugs of coffee and shoved aside the laden bags she'd brought, clearing a space on the scrubbed wooden table.

Sadie sat, pushing tomato-stained fingers through her short black hair. She looked a mess. Tomatoes stained hands and clothing a deep murky brown, and so she only wore her oldest, most worn and torn clothes. Today she wore a ratty singlet with paint on the nfront and a tear on one shoulder, its original pale yellow discolored by tomatoes. Her cut-off denim shorts were as brief as they were tight. The neatest thing about her was the pair of steel-toed work boots.

She sat opposite Erica and picked up the mug of coffee with a sigh.

"Tough morning?" Erica's eyes twinkled over the rim of her mug. A wicked glance that skated Sadie's face before sliding away. An instant of heat in the gaze, which, as it always did, made Sadie wonder if Erica was flirting with her.

"Yeah. It's always harder this time of year. It's an oven in the greenhouse by 8 a.m. so I'm here as soon as it's light. As Queensland's the Dinosaur State that doesn't believe in Daylight Saving, that means I'm at work by 4 a.m."

Erica nodded. "I was turning over in bed at 4 a.m., wishing the kookaburras would shut up so that I could get back to sleep. There's one in particular that sits in the tree right outside my window. I swear if I had a shotgun—"

"You'd aim and miss. Deliberately."

"Maybe. Maybe not. I couldn't get back to sleep, so I got up at 4:30 a.m. and made another batch of tomato sauce." She nodded at the bags on the edge of the table.

"Great. I think I sold the last of that yesterday. I've got money for you."

"I took a look at the shelves while I was waiting for the coffee to brew. You've sold all of my smoked sundried tomatoes and all but one jar of the green tomato chutney!"

"The smoked sundried tomatoes sold the first day. One of the restaurateurs took most of them, and the rest went soon after. If you can provide more, they could be a steady money-earner for you."

"For us," Erica corrected. "You supply the vine-ripe freshly picked tomatoes, I work my magic on them, and we go fifty-fifty. Did you get a chance to try them?"

Sadie shook her head. "No. They were sold too quickly."

"Make sure you put some aside next time. If I say it myself, they're bloody awesome!"

"You can have these two trays of tomatoes here, and there are another three trays of seconds around the back if you want them. Is that enough?"

"Perfect." Erica's face glowed with enthusiasm. "Thank you."

After coffee, Sadie helped Erica load the trays into the back of her shiny Lexus. Not for the first time, she wondered why a woman of such obvious affluence spent many hours each week making preserves for sale. Erica didn't look as if she needed the money. Their arrangement was an informal one—Sadie paid Erica her share of the takings when she saw her. She didn't even know where she lived, whom she lived with, or what she did with her day. To Sadie, Erica was a warm and witty woman who appeared a couple of times a week to share a chat and a coffee. But their conversation seldom touched on the personal. Sadie, whose gaydar was usually finely tuned, couldn't even be sure if Erica liked women. She thought she did, thought she picked up a hint of flirtation in their morning exchanges, but she didn't know, and she wasn't going to wreck a good working relationship on the off chance that Elegant Erica would want to go on a date with Scruffy Sadie.

The Lexus purred off. Sadie blew out her cheeks, lifted her sweaty singlet from her skin and walked back to the greenhouse to continue picking.

Erica appeared again two days later. Sadie was perched in front of the computer in the corner of the shed that passed for her office. Seeing the Lexus, she rose to put on a fresh pot of coffee. It would be a welcome break to talk with Erica, hear her animated voice discuss Tomato Kasundi and whether chilli and garlic enhanced the dried tomatoes or overpowered their flavor. Maybe, she decided, she would flirt just the tiniest bit. Strictly an experiment, of course, to see if Erica picked up on it. But not enough that she couldn't hit reverse if needed.

Like Sadie, Erica was wearing shorts and a singlet, although Erica's were pristine and bright, which displayed her lean, tanned limbs to great advantage. Sadie let her eyes linger on her thighs for a moment, captivated by their smooth firmness. It was too long a glance, as when her eyes returned to Erica's face, there was a little half-smile on Erica's lips, a knowing little expression, an acknowledgement of something shared. So Erica did like women. Sadie filed the information away, but pushed it aside. Someone like Erica still wouldn't date someone like her.

Erica set down her laden bags and started pulling things out. "Tomato Kasundi. Passata. I've put rosemary in this batch, and a dash of chilli—I think you'll like it. Smoked Sundried Tomatoes, of course. Oh, and Tomato and Passionfruit Jam."

Sadie couldn't help herself—her nose wrinkled at the thought. What a waste of perfectly good passionfruit.

Erica caught the look. "You don't like it? But it's an Aussie tradition! Everyone's granny used to make Tomato and Passionfruit Jam. I'll bet it sells. Here," and she dug around in her bags again. "I've made muffins to go with our coffee. You can try some on those."

"No, thanks."

But Erica had produced a knife, split one of the muffins and was spreading it lavishly with the jewel-red jam, studded with the dark passionfruit seeds. "Take it. At least try a bite before you turn your cute little nose up." Erica's own nose wrinkled charmingly and she flicked a glance at Sadie from under lowered lashes.

"Really. No. Just no."

"Why not?" Erica waved the muffin to and fro under Sadie's nose. "Just one teeny, tiny bite. One small nibble. A *soupçon*. And then if you don't like it, I'll put it on the shelf and never mention it again. At least not until I collect my money."

Sadie put some distance between herself and Erica's manicured fingers holding the morsel.

"Don't you like passionfruit?" Erica persisted.

"It's not the passionfruit."

"Then what? Is it too sweet for you?"

Sadie hesitated. It would be easy to nod and agree it was very sweet, but if she did that, Erica was likely to make a batch with more fruit and less sugar. More tomatoes. Then she'd be in this same predicament again.

She met Erica's eyes in wry shame. "The truth? I don't like tomatoes."

The muffin fell to the table unnoticed. Erica scooted closer and her hand cupped Sadie's chin. Her fingers were warm and dry despite the clinging humidity of the day.

"Did I hear you correctly?" Her fingers turned Sadie's face so she could look in her eyes. "You, the tomato lady of Tomato Lady Pty Ltd, the premier grower of gourmet tomatoes on the Coast, the lady whose tomatoes win prizes, awards, and are sought after by Michelin five-star restaurants and home cooks alike, do not like tomatoes?"

Caught in Erica's intense gaze, Sadie could only manage the tiniest of nods. She rarely told anyone this. It wasn't good PR for the Tomato Lady to loathe the things.

Erica's fingers dropped away. "Are you allergic to them? Are you arthritic? Do you have an inflammatory condition?"

"No. I just don't like the taste."

"So you've never tried anything I've made?"

Shamed, Sadie shook her head.

"This won't do. What are you doing tomorrow night?"

"The same as I do every night. Early dinner, early to bed. I rise at 3:30 a.m."

"Then we'll make it early." Erica dug in her bag, producing a scrap of paper and a pen, and scribbled something down. "My address. I'll expect you for dinner at 5 p.m. Is that early enough for you? We'll have you in bed by eight."

Startled, Sadie's eyes flew to the other woman's face. The glimmer of humor she saw told her the wording had been intentional, designed to tease.

"I'll cook a tomato feast, and I guarantee that you'll like it."

"You're not the first to have tried this. Really, Erica, your wonderful cooking would be wasted on me."

"How do you know it's wonderful if you've never tried it? It's a date."

"A date," Sadie said faintly. Was Erica reading her mind? A vision seeped into her head of a romantic dinner for two, a fine bottle of wine, candles maybe, on a patio under the stars in the warm Queensland evening. Her heart and other regions purred in anticipation.

"A date," said Erica firmly. "You can bring the wine."

Sadie grinned, something anticipatory and warm spreading deep in her belly. "Red or white?"

"One of each. My tomato feast will need the proper accompaniment."

The tomatoes. Some of the light went out of the morning. Sadie hoped that Erica wouldn't be too mortified when her feast went virtually untouched.

Sadie arrived at Erica's at 5 p.m. the next day. She lived in a surprisingly modest weatherboard Queenslander, set high to catch the breeze on the ridge. Sadie parked her van next to Erica's Lexus and found the stairs to the verandah. She carried a bag of her finest Lavanzo tomatoes, round, rich and red, bursting with flavor, as well as two bottles of wine.

Erica met her at the top of the stairs, and took the wine and tomatoes from her hands. "Welcome."

The verandah faced north, and the late afternoon sun was filtered by a screen. It was a homey space, crammed with herbs in pots, a Balinese lounger on which sprawled a black and white cat, and a round wooden table set for two. The view stretched to the north, over canefields to the range behind. A lazy fan created a pleasing movement of air.

Erica disappeared inside the house and reappeared a moment later with two glasses of bubbles. "Cheers," she said, clinking glasses. She stood at the rail, close enough that Sadie quivered.

Since Erica's unexpected invitation, she'd thought of little else. If Sadie had any doubts that she was reading the invitation wrong, they were set aside when Erica touched her hand, her fingers lingering a moment too long for friendship.

"I'm glad you're here," said Erica. "I've wanted to ask you for a long time."

"Need advice on your tomatoes?"

Erica snorted. "As if. Why do I need to grow them when the best tomatoes in Australia are just down the road? Sit." She indicated the Balinese lounge. "Let me feed you."

Erica gestured toward a large plate set on a low table in front of the lounge. "I'm starting you off gently. This is my homemade goat cheese, topped with a slice of smoked sundried tomato, basil from the garden drizzled with balsamic glaze. If you're feeling particularly carnivorous, salami from the local butcher, and smoked Kalamata olives." She grinned. "No tomatoes in those. I need a back-up in case you do hate my tomato feast."

Sadie studied the plate. It wasn't that she couldn't eat tomatoes. When she had first bought the farm, she had gorged on them almost to the exclusion of everything else.

Tomatoes for breakfast, lunch, and dinner. Now they held zero appeal. If it was a choice between a tomato sandwich and plain bread, she'd eat the dry bread without complaint.

The goat cheese looked tempting, and the tomato topping was scanty. She took a bite, letting the mild cheese coat her tongue, mingling with the fresh basil, and, yes, an explosion of taste from the sundried tomato. It wasn't overwhelming—the tomato blended in with the other flavors to create a mouthful of heaven.

Erica watched her closely. "Still alive?"

"Um." Sadie reached for a second one, wondering if it could be as delicious. It was.

Erica lowered herself to the lounge next to Sadie. "Eat up. You obviously don't need to worry about calories, and I love it when people enjoy my cooking."

"It's the physical work." Sadie reached for another cracker with goat cheese and licked the crumbs from her lips. With a jolt, she realized Erica was watching her, her eyes following the path of Sadie's tongue as it swept around casting for stray crumbs. The look wasn't that of a friend, it was that of a potential lover. Something sweet and heavy settled in the pit of Sadie's belly, the warmth radiating outward. Erica wanted her.

And she wanted Erica.

"Why do you make the tomato products?" she asked. It wasn't what she wanted to say, but it was a start.

"Because I don't look as if I need the money?" Erica's lips twisted wryly. "So many people think that. I have this house, I drive a Lexus. But the Lexus is twelve years old and this house is all I got from my ex-husband. He divorced me," she continued, in answer to Sadie's unspoken question.

"Jeff didn't like me working and heaven knows he made enough money that I didn't need to. I didn't have a career to fall back on when we split, but I needed an income. So I started making baked goods and selling them at the farmers' markets. But if I didn't sell them all they were wasted, and there's only so much banana bread I can eat. So I switched to preserves. I'm doing okay now, mainly thanks to the Tomato Lady."

Was this meal a thank you? The glow of anticipation dimmed, but then Erica touched her hand, a light press of her fingers, and a slow sweep of her thumb.

"That's not why I invited you. Don't think that, Sadie."

The little flame was still burning, and now it was a bit brighter. "You want to convert me into a tomato lover."

"That, too." Erica rose. "I'll leave you with the last of these. I'm going to toss the salad."

Sadie relaxed into the cushions, petting the black and white cat, which purred in response. She was comfortable here, on Erica's lounge, eating Erica's food, stroking Erica's cat. A small sigh. It had been so long since she'd had a lover. Long antisocial hours and rural living put her out of the orbit of most potential partners. Maybe she and Erica would tread that road. Maybe.

Her musing was cut short by Erica's appearance with a flat dish. She set it in the center of the table and bustled away before reappearing with salad and the bottle of red wine.

Sadie moved to the table, her mouth watering. It looked like lasagna—something she could eat, as the beef and cheese were enough to counteract the dreaded taste of tomatoes.

Erica sat opposite her and nudged the hot dish in Sadie's direction. "Help yourself. Moussaka is one of my specialties. I hope you enjoy it."

Sadie's hand hovered over the dish. Moussaka. The classic Greek dish was a blend of lamb and tomato, flavored with oregano. And eggplant—her most hated vegetable after tomatoes. Soggy, almost slimy, with a very distinctive flavor, one she definitely hadn't acquired a taste for. But the smell of baked cheese and lamb was alluring. Sadie scooped a small amount onto her plate and helped herself to the salad, which contained thick slices of ripe tomato, torn basil leaves, and fresh buffalo mozzarella.

Erica poured red wine, and brushed away the black and white cat when it tried to jump onto her lap. Sadie picked at her own plate, savoring the cheese topping and the lamb, and avoiding the eggplant, while she watched Erica eat. There was a sensuousness to her eating, a seriousness. Erica ate with steady concentration, each mouthful appreciated fully before swallowing and followed by a taste of wine.

"You're staring." Erica put down her fork. "Am I chewing with my mouth open?"

"I enjoy watching you eat. There's such pleasure in every mouthful."

"Too much pleasure, according to Jeff." Erica wrinkled her nose in disgust. "He was always trying to change me. So I found someone who loved me as I was. I ran off with his secretary. Jeff couldn't take the double whammy of being left, and being left for a woman. I was lucky to get enough from him to buy this house."

Sadie grinned at the disgusted tone of Erica's voice.

Erica took another bite of her moussaka and gestured with her wine glass. "You're not eating much. Don't you like moussaka?" She leaned closer, peering into Sadie's eyes. "Don't tell me it's too tomatoey? It's okay, you can tell me. I won't be offended."

Sadie closed her eyes in mortification. Now she had to admit it wasn't just tomatoes; she was an unadventurous eater. Erica, who obviously adored creative cooking, would be disgusted.

Erica sat back. "Let me tell you what's going through your head. Over the last week you've wondered if I like women. You've been trying to decide if I was flirting with you. Then you wondered what a rich bitch like me would want with a tomato farmer like you. Add a sprinkling of shame that you would rather eat dirt than tomatoes, and embarrassment that you're not appreciating my very fine cooking this evening. Throw in a side dish of angst about losing a friendship and a working relationship if it all goes wrong." She took a sip of wine. "Have I covered it?"

"I think you got most of it." Sadie twisted her hands in her lap. She wasn't sure exactly when she'd become so inept in a dating situation, but she was as clueless here as she was when she was fifteen and trying to ask her best friend on a date, a real date. Come to think of it, that hadn't ended well, either.

Erica leaned forward. A wisp of hair brushed her cheek, accentuating her high cheekbones. "Forget the food." At Sadie's startled look, she added, "It's not about the food or my cooking. That was an excuse. I would have asked you out anyway, as soon as I'd worked up my courage. I had a list of casual invitations to use on you. It went something like 'dinner at my place, the Sunday beach markets, trip to the food and wine festival.' And the big one of course."

She had to ask. "Which is?"

"I know you do the local farmer's market on Saturdays. I was going to suggest we join forces and I include some of my products on your stall. Then I was going to drop them around to your place one Friday evening. You'd offer me a glass of wine, we'd get chatting, I'd have another glass and another and then I'd be over the limit and unable to drive home. You'd offer me the couch." She twiddled the stem of her wine glass. "My fantasy takes off from there."

Sadie swallowed. Seldom had she been given the gift of such honest intent. Her past dates had been couched in spur of the moment desire and too much wine. Here and now, they were both sober, and Erica's intentions were out in the open, hanging freely for her to accept. She reached over the table and took the other woman's hand, turning it over and studying the contrast. Erica's hand was soft, white, and cared for, with square-cut manicured nails painted with clear polish. Her own hand was hard and tanned, brown with sun and a faint tinge of tomato stain that never completely disappeared.

"You read my mind. That's exactly what I thought—that you were out of my league and I shouldn't go there anyway. Business and pleasure—a sad, bad mix."

"Then there's the whole food thing." Erica clasped Sadie's hand firmly, linked their fingers together. "Look at me, Sadie."

When Sadie complied, Erica stated, "I am more than food. Go on, repeat it aloud if you have to, but make sure it sinks in. You don't like tomatoes? No problem. You want to eat steak and chips every night? We'll work around it. Just as we'll work around your early-to-bed habits. If we want to, we can do this."

There was a strange, sad expression on Erica's face, as if she were expecting to be knocked back. Maybe she thought

Sadie didn't want her. Whatever the outcome, Sadie couldn't let her think that. Drawing a deep breath, she tugged Erica's hand, pulling her closer. "Aren't we getting a little ahead of ourselves? We're planning the parameters of our relationship and we haven't even kissed."

A smile broke over Erica's face. "I wasn't going to make you sign a contract. And even if I were, a kiss is the best way I know to seal one."

They each moved forward, knees bumping, then when they couldn't get closer with the table in the way, they stood. Sadie's hand on Erica's waist. Erica's hand curving around Sadie's neck. Their faces were close now, enough that Sadie felt the soft puff of Erica's breath on her face, the tang of wine on her breath, and the scent of citrus soap. Then they were kissing, lips meeting, tentatively at first, then firmer, with delight and joy, and the restraints fell away.

Disbelief and exhilaration twined together in Sadie's head. To think she had gotten to this point with Erica. To think there was so much more to come. Oh, so much more. The scenarios flashed through her head: first dinner in a restaurant, first lovemaking, first time to wake in the morning, entwined in bed, arms and legs in a knot. Meeting each other's friends and family. Planning a life together.

The scenarios flickered and drifted away, stored in memory to be brought out and examined another time, another less frenetic time. Now there was the here-and-now, a moment to be treasured, experienced, and then filed away labeled "First Kiss." A memory to revisit often.

Erica's tongue swept around Sadie's mouth, taunting and tasting. There was heat and moisture, wine, and desire. When they pulled apart to breathe, Sadie was panting with exhilaration and desire.

Even when the kiss was over, it wasn't finished. There were nuzzles and pecks, gentle touches to cheek, corner of lips, and eye. Sadie learned how Erica felt under her fingers, mapped the contours of her cheeks, studied the way her erratic pulse thundered in her slim neck and the uneven bump on her left collarbone. And in turn, she shivered at the touch of Erica's lips in the hollow of her throat and her fingers on her bare arm, learning the bumps of elbow, the hardness of muscles.

Sadie forgot about dinner, about eggplant and tomato, the fact she had to rise at 3:30 a.m. There was only Erica: in her head, under her hands, and soon, she knew, in her heart.

It was only when the black and white cat leaped onto the table and then onto Erica's shoulder, her tail in Sadie's face, that they broke apart.

Sadie searched Erica's face. The happiness that shone there, she knew, must be mirrored in her own. Erica removed the cat from her shoulder and set it down. It stalked off, tail quivering, and jumped onto the lounge, where it curled onto a cushion and watched them through slitted green eyes.

"We have a choice." Erica picked up Sadie's hand, as if she couldn't form the words without the contact. "The first is I walk you to your van, we kiss goodnight, and you drive away, home to your lonely bed." Her eyes crinkled at the corners. "You do have to rise at 3:30 a.m., I believe?"

Sadie smiled back, the joy and anticipation thrumming in her veins. "And the alternative?"

"The second is I walk you to my bedroom, and we kiss as the prelude to more. And at 3:30 a.m. you rise, and I'll make coffee while you shower."

Sadie entwined her fingers with Erica's and asked, "Where's your bedroom?"

This time when they kissed, it was with the knowledge that it didn't have to end. In Erica's high-ceilinged bedroom, under the slow whop-whop of the ceiling fan, they removed each other's clothes, piece by piece, stopping to explore each new area of skin as it was revealed.

Erica was lean, freckled white where the sun didn't touch. Her breasts were small, rose-tipped, and if there was a softness due to age, then Sadie embraced it, as it was part of the woman that was Erica. Her own body was harder, firmer, with muscles used to physical work. Browner, too, from the sun. When they lay together on Erica's silver-green quilt, when they entwined their legs, the contrast between their bodies was an added delight.

Sadie slipped two fingers into Erica's pussy, reveling in the moisture, and slid them slowly in and out, and the delight on the older woman's face increased her own pleasure. When she lay between her spread thighs, when she reached for the first, heady taste, she was light-headed with euphoria.

Erica reciprocated, learning the valleys and curves of Sadie's body, learning her taste, and sharing it with a finger to Sadie's lips.

Erica came first under Sadie's fingers, then by her tongue, and then silently a third time. They learned each other, what they liked, what was less pleasurable. Sadie found that Erica was a gasper, a panter, and when her orgasm hit, she keened a high, winding note that was almost like a song.

Sadie was quiet, directing the pleasure inward, her eyes closed to focus on how it felt, her pleasure all through touch and scent. Her climax built in a slow expansion that exploded in white light behind her eyes, made her belly clench, as the ripples spread outward, like a stone thrown in water.

It was late when, finally sated, they curled up together on the big bed. Sadie kissed the salt from Erica's breast, rested her head on her lover's shoulder and sighed. A deep sigh. Not asleep yet, but not too far away.

Erica kissed the top of her head, and wrapped her arm around her.

A stray thought wound its way through Sadie's head. "We never had dessert," she said.

Erica chuckled. "That's probably a good thing."

It was hard to form the words in the thickness of impending sleep. "What was it?"

"Tomato and ginger ice cream."

ERICA'S TOMATO SAUCE

Directions
All quantities are approximate—you
can adapt to your own taste.

1. Take 2 kilograms of overripe vine-ripened tomatoes, and a bunch of fresh herbs (oregano, basil, rosemary, a small amount of parsley). Quarter the tomatoes then place in a food processor with the herbs and process until nearly smooth.

2. Measure the mixture into a saucepan. For every cup of processed tomatoes, add 1 tablespoon of brown sugar, 1 teaspoon of salt, and 2 tablespoons of store-bought tomato puree. Bring to the boil and simmer until reduced by half.

3. Place into sterilized jars and close the lid tightly. Reverse the jars, standing each on its lid for a couple of minutes. This sucks the air out of the jars and enhances keeping qualities.

4. Place the jars right side up in a large saucepan and add enough boiling water so that the water comes halfway up the side of the jars. "Process" the sauce by boiling for 10 minutes.

5. Unopened jars will keep in a cupboard for 3 months. Once opened, store in the refrigerator and use within 3 days.

6. For an easy dinner, stir the sauce through cooked pasta. Use as a base for chilli or Bolognese sauce. Pan-fry crumbed chicken schnitzels, top with a thick layer of sauce and grated cheese, then bake in a hot oven for 10 minutes to make Chicken Parmigiana. Add a touch of chilli and toss through diced, roasted potatoes to make Patatas Bravas.

EAST MEETS WEST

KARIS WALSH

CHICKEN FRIED STEAK WITH MASHED *potatoes and gravy*. Rena sighed. Why did *every* restaurant in Texas—no matter what type of food it served—have this disgusting concoction on the menu? Bland and greasy. Instead, she ordered chipotle chicken enchiladas and a pineapple-jalapeño margarita, the most flavorful options she could find. When the waiter left their table, her co-workers continued their discussion about brutal work hours while Rena leaned back in her chair and gazed idly around the garish cantina.

She still couldn't believe she was living in San Antonio. Permanently and irrevocably. She had followed her family's advice in so many matters over the years. Get straight As in school, come to America for her college education, complete her medical degree at Stanford, intern at a prestigious West Coast hospital. She had been content to make her parents happy, as long as their ambitions aligned with her own. But, try as she might, she hadn't been able to reconcile herself to the next steps they had laid out for her. Return to India for an elaborate and arranged marriage to a suitable guy and then settle down to raise a family while putting her career in obstetrics on hold. Work for years on a degree just to be considered more attractive to potential mates? Where was the logic in that?

Her attention fell on a woman sitting at the bar drinking a beer. The other reason Rena had needed to find the strength to resist years of conditioning by her parents and society was because she couldn't live a lie for the rest of her life. She couldn't play the happy wife and mother when she wanted to be independent and working and—most important—able to choose the gender of a partner based on her own desires and preferences, not on the expectations of her traditional family.

The woman on the barstool was exactly the type Rena would choose, too. Sexy, with a defiant confidence Rena didn't possess but that she found irresistibly alluring. Her jeans had a barbed-wire motif stitched across the back pockets, and her white dress shirt looked crisply ironed. A black cowboy hat sat on the bar next to her arm, and when she crossed her legs, light glinted off a chain wrapped around the ankle of her dusty black cowboy boots. Rena took a long drink from her water glass, her mouth suddenly dry. She had never seen someone wear jewelry on an old boot before—and where else but Texas would anyone think to do it?

She was trying to figure out why the combination of bright silver filigree chain against worn boot leather was such a huge turn-on when the woman shifted to give a waitress room to put a plate of food in front of her. Rena's disappointment that the object of her momentary infatuation had ordered chicken fried steak was short-lived once she saw her face. Short chestnut hair tucked behind her ears, blue eyes the color of a cold mountain stream. Classically beautiful proportions that would have seemed attractive in a superficial way if it hadn't been for the glow of a summer tan across her cheekbones and nose. The color of a ripe and juicy mango. Rena wanted a bite.

Her cheeks warmed when the woman smiled at her and raised her glass in a silent salute. Rena turned away without returning the smile and took a long sip of the chilly margarita the waiter had brought. Crushed ice melted instantly on her tongue, and gentle heat from the jalapeños warmed her throat. She licked her lips—sweet with the taste of pineapple—and wondered if she only imagined the physical sensation of the woman's eyes on her. Although she refused to look at the bar again, she was internally focused on the woman sitting there. She pictured her eating, her tongue sliding out of her mouth to catch an errant drop of creamy gravy…

Rena sighed and forced herself to join the conversation at her table. She had managed to defy her family by accepting a job at a clinic in Texas instead of flying home to begin meeting suitors, and by telling them she was gay. But her courage only stretched so far. Definitely not far enough for her to be able to walk up to a complete stranger and proposition her.

She took a bite of enchilada with smoky chipotle sauce. The heat from the peppers was dulled by the heavy dose of sour cream in the sauce. Rena had agreed to join her friends for a rare night out, but she'd much rather be eating alone at home. Chicken coated in cumin, coriander, and turmeric. A cooling cucumber raita instead of the heavy sour cream. Plum chutney and basmati studded with currants and cashews instead of the goopy beans and tasteless rice on her plate.

Even though she had stood up to her parents, she was still living a version of the same life she had known since childhood. She cooked and ate familiar Indian dishes at home, surrounded by family heirlooms. Once she was inside her apartment, she might as well have been in India, but she was reluctant to change. She was adjusting to her new home—comfortable in the heat and appreciating the strange, sparse beauty of her surroundings—but she couldn't get herself to like the food. Tex-Mex, Mexican, steaks, super-sized takeout burgers—nothing in Texas seemed to appeal to her palate. Rena checked out the woman at the bar once more. Well, she did find something—make that *someone*—appealing.

But telling her family she had chosen a different way of life and actually *living* the new way of life were two very different things.

Rena's group splintered as they passed by some boutique shops. Two went into a trendy clothing store while the other pair stopped to buy ice cream. Rena sat down on a bench and watched a mother duck herd her ducklings near the bank. She had been distracted during dinner, unable to follow the threads of conversation around her, because her thoughts were consumed by the woman she had seen. She needed a few minutes to pull herself together, but she worried that it would take a dip in the cool river to completely douse her arousal.

"Mind if I join you?"

Rena started as her fantasy woman—in reality only a yard away—spoke to her. Her down-home Texas accent was rich and sweet. "Um, no. I suppose it's okay." She scooted over a few inches and waved stiffly toward the bench.

"My name is Liz." She held out her hand for Rena to shake, and then she sat down.

"I'm Rena." Her own voice, usually cultured and precise, seemed determined to betray her attraction to Liz, and she was only able to force out brief, awkward sentences. She rubbed her hand on her thigh, although she wasn't sure whether she was trying to erase the tingling sensation caused by Liz's firm grip or if she wanted to spread the feeling to the rest of her body.

"I have to confess that I followed you from the cantina." Liz rested her elbows on her knees and fidgeted with her cowboy hat, wiping at a smudge of dirt on the black felt. She appeared almost as awkward and hesitant as Rena felt, and the realization gave Rena a boost in confidence. She had been so concerned about her attraction to a stranger that she hadn't stopped to consider that the stranger might be interested in *her* as well.

"I wanted a chance to meet you. I hope you don't mind," Liz added.

"Not at all," Rena said. "I—I noticed you, too. At the bar."

Liz smiled. "Where are you from?"

Rena hesitated for a brief moment. Liz's smooth drawl had momentarily emptied her mind of any coherent thought. "From India," she said. Duh. She struggled to gather her wandering thoughts and string together more words. "I grew up in the province of Assam, near Jorhat. My parents own a tea plantation there."

"Really? That must have been fascinating. I love tea."

Rena answered Liz's smile with one of her own. She wasn't sure if Liz drank anything besides the sweetened iced tea ubiquitous in this part of the country, but Rena suddenly wanted the opportunity to introduce her to the subtle nuances of flavor from her childhood. She shifted on the bench, putting another inch or two between them. Liz was simply being friendly, stopping to chat, and Rena had them visiting India, sampling tea, meeting her parents. Was she so desperate for a relationship that she'd invent one with so little provocation? She pushed aside the appealing image of Liz, sweaty in the humid heights of Assam and with a delicate cup of tea in her slender, work-roughened fingers.

"Yes, it was fascinating," Rena agreed. Usually recalcitrant about her childhood, she wanted to talk to Liz about swinging like a monkey through the trees on her parents' estate, learning each step of the intricate process of drying and blending tea leaves, and struggling to balance her growing independence and sexual identity in a land ruled by custom and obedience, but she kept her thoughts to herself. "But I came to the States for college and now I'm planning to live here permanently. Are you originally from Texas?"

"Did my accent give me away?" Liz laughed. "My parents own a ranch just outside of San Antonio, and I've always lived here. I studied agricultural science at A&M and I'm the ranch manager now. How do you like Texas so far?"

Rena wanted to keep talking about Liz. About her desire to stay close to her family while Rena had struggled so hard to break free. But she accepted the change to a less comfortable topic of conversation.

"I think it's beautiful here, and the people are friendly," she said. "Plus, I love my job. But I just can't get used to the food. It's usually so heavy and the portions are huge!"

"Everything's bigger in Texas," Liz said with a laugh.

Rena laughed, too. She had been feeling homesick and guilty since her move to Texas, and the feelings had grown each time she had tried the local cuisine and dismissed it as inferior to what she had known at home. Her inability to adapt had made her doubt her decision at times, but Liz's laughter lightened her mood.

"I was at a fast food restaurant the other day, and I swear I heard the man in front of me ask to have his meal waddle-sized. Did that mean he got so much food he'd waddle back to his car?"

Liz laughed harder. "I think he must have said 'what-a-sized'. But the result is the same." She wiped her eyes on her shirt sleeve and looked across the courtyard before she stood up. "Your friends are coming back, so I should let you get back to your evening."

Rena swallowed her disappointment and held out her hand for Liz to shake again. She had just started to relax in Liz's company, feeling a glimmer of hope that this conversation might lead to a future date. Maybe a friendship, or something more. "I enjoyed meeting you, Liz."

Liz kept hold of her hand and tugged gently, pulling Rena to her feet. "Me, too, Rena."

Rena wanted to linger with the feeling of Liz's fingers wrapped around her own. Warm and rough and firm. She reluctantly tried to disengage their hands, but Liz didn't let go. "Come riding with me sometime? I'll give you a tour of the ranch. You must miss the open spaces now that you're living in the city. Then I'll cook you a meal that will make you fall in love with the taste of Texas."

Rena's instinct was to say no, to walk away from the heady fantasy of standing in Liz's kitchen while she cooked.

Maybe they'd feed each other with their fingers, use mouths and tongues on skin as much as on the food, and then move from the table to the bedroom... Rena's dreams were too much romance novel and too little rooted in reality, but she pulled her hand free and slipped a business card out of her back pocket.

"I'd like that," she said. "Call me sometime."

Rena walked toward her coworkers, her hands shaking from the contact with Liz. A date? A chance to see Liz again? She had kept her voice casual when she handed over her card, but heat was building inside her. She hoped Liz would call her soon because no matter what she was planning to cook, Rena was more than ready to eat.

"Have a seat," Liz said, pulling out a barstool for Rena when they entered Liz's small farmhouse kitchen. "I'll get you a glass of wine and start cooking."

Rena perched on the leather-covered stool. She was already cooking inside. Her blood had been simmering since she and Liz had talked on the River Walk, and today's activities had brought her to a full boil. A long ride on gentle Quarter Horses past grazing longhorns and feathery-green mesquite trees. A quick stop by the main ranch house, where Rena had met Liz's parents. They had seemed as surprised to meet her as she was to be introduced. Throughout the day, there had been casual touches and lingering glances. Nothing overly intimate, but Rena had felt each brush of Liz's hands as keenly as if she was being seared in a hot pan. Her skin felt almost bruised by the soft pressure of fingers against her back guiding her on a tour of the ranch house, along her leg as Liz adjusted her stirrups before their ride.

Liz pulled the cork out of a bottle and poured a deep ruby wine into two glasses. She handed one to Rena and held up her own.

"To food. Old tastes and new flavors. Both ought to be savored." Liz clinked the rim of her glass against Rena's and took a drink of wine. "This is a Cabernet made from grapes grown in a vineyard near Lubbock. I hope you like it."

Rena took a sip. Deep and complex, like Liz. And tasty, also like Liz. Rena had known she was attracted to Liz's appearance, to her work-roughened, sun-tinted beauty, from first glance. But Rena had seen more of Liz today. Her innovative approaches to ranching and her inquisitive intelligence. Her willingness to try new methods and her love of her family and their traditions. Old and new, like the shiny silver against her stained old boots. Beauty in layers.

"It's delicious," Rena said. She leaned her elbows on the counter and watched Liz collect ingredients from her pantry and fridge. She had been expecting a traditional Western barbecue or a Tex-Mex plate of tamales and burritos, and she'd been determined to eat whatever Liz made without comparing it to the dishes she'd known since childhood. But chicken fried steak? What genuine and believable compliment would she be able to give after eating it?

"What are you making?" she asked, hoping she'd guessed wrong and Liz was cooking something more palatable. Like maybe shoe leather.

"Chicken fried steak," she said, dashing Rena's hope for a less offensive meal. "You've probably noticed how popular it is in Texas. But this version has a twist, just for you."

Rena sipped her wine as Liz started to cook. They had talked easily all day, sharing stories from their childhoods and comparing their experiences in school and in dating, but they fell silent as Liz focused on her meal. Rena watched with growing interest as Liz seasoned some flour with curry powder and coated thin steaks with the bright yellow mixture. She fried them in a shallow pool of grapeseed oil before putting them in the oven to stay warm. She heated some cumin seeds in the hot oil, then added a little flour and stirred in some broth. She seasoned the thickening gravy with garam masala and ground black pepper and finished it with a dash of cream, fresh chopped cilantro, and a generous squeeze of lime juice.

Rena sat still as Liz came around the counter and stood behind her, putting her arms around Rena's waist. Rena leaned back against her, inhaling Liz's perfectly blended and complex perfume of spice and horse and sunshine. Liz placed gentle kisses from Rena's collarbone and along her neck to her ear lobe. She softly nibbled on Rena's ear.

"Are you ready to eat?"

"Yes," Rena said simply, hoping Liz's question meant more than dinner. She sighed when Liz stepped away from her and led the way to the table. She held out a chair for Rena before going back to the kitchen.

Rena stared at the Texas-sized plate of food in front of her. The curry-scented steak sat on top of a generous scoop of basmati rice. Aromatic gravy flecked with green cilantro dripped down the sides of the steak and soaked into the rice. Mango-pecan chutney and a cooling salad made from shredded cabbage and avocado in a yogurt dressing rounded out the meal.

"It's not authentic Indian food and it isn't exactly traditional Texan, but maybe the combination will work."

Rena could only nod in response, awed by the thought and care Liz had put into this meal and by the meaning behind the food. She took a bite and tasted the warmth of familiar spices and the unfamiliar textures of fried steak and crispy coating. The flavor of pecans dominated the chutney, making a condiment she'd eaten since she was a baby suddenly new and startling. The food represented the new life she wanted for herself—one full of respect for both her culture and her individual dreams. Liz had shown her how the flavors of her old and new worlds could be blended in the kitchen, but Rena was the only one who could make the same magic happen in her life. She picked up a piece of creamy avocado with her fingers and leaned across the table to raise her fingers to Liz's lips.

Rena gasped quietly when Liz opened her mouth and ate the bite she offered, using her tongue to lick the yogurt sauce off her fingers. Ever since Liz's phone call, Rena had tried to imagine how this day would go. She had hoped the afternoon together would lead to a night spent in each other's arms, even though she had expected to feel embarrassed by her inexperience and need for Liz to take the lead. But Liz's cooking had proved something to her. Liz wasn't trying to change her or expect her to be anything other than who she was—instead, she was interested in finding out what the two of them could be when combined, blended, heated. Rena made the first move and walked over to her chair.

"Your cooking is amazing," Rena said as she knelt between Liz's knees and leaned her head against Liz's thigh.

"I love that you did this for me, that you brought some of my culture into yours."

Rena felt Liz's fingers tremble as they stroked her hair. "And I loved making this for you. Showing you what could happen when you opened yourself to the local cuisine."

Rena lifted her head for a kiss, her fingers digging into Liz's thighs. "I know exactly what I want for dessert," Rena said. She teased Liz's lips with her tongue. "Something—some*one* local, sweet, and oh, so delicious."

She slid her tongue into Liz's mouth, gently probing and exploring. Liz moaned, and the intensity of the sound resonated through Rena and connected them. East and west. Different cultures, different lifestyles, but somehow a magical blend like the spices from Liz's meal.

She unzipped Liz's jeans and tugged them down, surprised at her own boldness but reveling in it, too. She closed her eyes and inhaled as the scent of Liz's arousal overpowered everything in Rena's mind, from the aroma of curry to her own inhibitions and concerns. She lowered her head and tentatively used her tongue to taste Liz. Hot and wet, earthy and new. Liz's fingers ceased their gentle stroking and curled tightly in Rena's hair. The more deeply Rena delved into Liz's wet folds, the shallower Liz's breathing became.

Rena moved with the small thrusts of Liz's hips, encouraging and inciting more motion as she licked and sucked. She kept one hand on Liz's inner thigh and dropped the other to Liz's ankle, securing their bodies together. Her fingers rested on the worn cowboy boot with its glittering bit of bling. Old and new. Balanced and without limits.

Rena held on tightly as Liz came in her mouth with a shuddering cry. Rena lingered, savoring the taste and feel of her new lover, until Liz leaned over and wrapped her arms around Rena, enveloping her in a sense of pulsating peace. Rena smiled and rested her cheek against Liz's belly. Something had shattered inside her during Liz's orgasm: limited thinking. A world of either-ors. Suddenly, Rena was ready for the future and all the new flavors it would bring.

She felt Liz's teeth graze the nape of her neck and her body responded to the teasing touch. "I hope you enjoyed your dinner," Liz said as she got up and urged Rena to her feet. She led them toward the bedroom. "Because I know I'm going to love dessert."

CURRIED CHICKEN FRIED STEAK

Ingredients

1 cup all-purpose flour

1 cup chickpea flour

2 teaspoons baking powder

1 teaspoon baking soda

3 tablespoons curry powder

salt and pepper to taste

2 eggs

1 cup buttermilk

4 cube steaks, pounded to ¼-inch thickness

grapeseed oil

Gravy:

1 tablespoon cumin seeds

5 tablespoons flour

1 tablespoon garam masala

½ teaspoon turmeric

½ teaspoon ground coriander

2 cups chicken broth

½ cup yogurt or sour cream (more if you want a creamier gravy)

¼ cup cilantro

juice of one fresh lime

Directions

1. Stir together flours, baking powder, baking soda, curry powder, salt, and freshly ground pepper.

2. In another bowl, beat eggs and buttermilk.

3. Dip the steaks in the flour mixture, then the egg mixture, then in the flour mixture again. Be sure to coat thoroughly.

4. Heat ½-inch of oil to 325 degrees F in a heavy pan and fry the steaks until brown, about 5 minutes per side. Remove them from pan, drain on paper towels, and keep warm in a low oven.

5. Pour off all but 5 tablespoons of oil from the pan (keep the browned bits on the bottom!) and add cumin seeds. Cook over medium heat until fragrant, and then sprinkle the flour and spices over the oil. Whisk until pale brown. Add the broth and deglaze the pan by scraping the yummy browned bits off the bottom. Bring to a boil and cook until thickened, stirring often.

6. Add the yogurt or sour cream and cilantro. Finish with fresh lime juice.

7. Serve steaks and gravy over basmati or jasmine rice.

DESSERT PLATTER

VICTORIA OLDHAM

THE ROOM WAS DIMLY LIT, and soft instrumental music played in the background. Diners sat at long communal tables, talking quietly. The boutique establishment, listed as a space for "sensual experiences with food", was the hottest new lesbian place in town, the tasteful, classy dark wood décor a perfect complement to the subtle aromas in the air. Teresa looked around, anticipation buzzing along her veins. She spotted her date in the far back of the room, speaking to a large butch woman wearing a frilly cook's apron. Cree saw her over the cook's shoulder and waved her back.

Teresa made her way through the restaurant, fascinated by the varied dishes on the tables, all of which were bright and multitextured. Most she didn't even recognize, but the smells in the room made her salivate. But nothing made her salivate like the woman in front of her. Cree's solid, muscular build, the tats that crawled up her arms like living vines, her swagger and kick-ass attitude—it was a heady combination that brought Teresa to her knees constantly, something they both enjoyed immensely.

"Hey, handsome," she said, giving Cree a kiss on the cheek.

"Hey, yourself, beautiful. Ready for an unusual night?" Cree draped her arm around Teresa's waist and she loved the feel of it. They'd only been dating a while, but already there was a calm familiarity, a general sense of trust and romance.

"I think so. Are we eating here?"

Cree pulled her tight and glanced at the woman she'd been talking to, who flashed a smile and disappeared through the swinging doors to the kitchen. She swept Teresa's hair away from her face and gave it a tug, making Teresa hiss softly in pleasure. Cree knew her buttons. "Do you remember telling me how much you loved food when we first started talking? And how erotic you found it?"

Teresa flushed and remembered that it had also been the night Cree had shown her how she could tie a cherry stem into a knot with her tongue, a tongue she had put to good use later. "I do. What about it?"

Cree brushed her lips against Teresa's, so feather soft it sent a chill up Teresa's spine. "I've set up a bit of something I want you to try tonight. Something I'm damn sure you haven't done before, but I think you'll enjoy. I sure as hell will." Her hand slid up the side of Teresa's breast, her thumb caressing the hard nipple.

She tried not to moan, aware that they were in a room full of people. "You know I'm up for just about anything. Lead the way." She stood on her tip-toes and bit Cree's full bottom lip, hard enough to be more than playful. She loved the way Cree's eyes darkened with desire and her grip around her waist tightened.

"Slow down, sugar, or I'm going to have to take you home, and you won't get your surprise. Come on." She took Teresa's hand and led her down a corridor glowing under black lights to another room. There was a low, long table in the middle, surrounded by various overstuffed pillows on the floor and a single overstuffed chair sat close to the head of the table. Shadows from candlelight played on the walls like erotic dancers, but other than that, the room was empty. Teresa gave Cree a questioning look.

"Trust me?" Cree's hand closed softly over Teresa's throat as she kissed her deeply, her look searching.

Teresa barely hesitated. All she'd learned about this woman over the last few months told her there was nothing to fear, and plenty to anticipate. "Yes. I do, actually."

Cree's smile was genuine and open, and laced with lust. "Good. Close your eyes."

Teresa did as she was told and shivered when the cool silk blindfold slid over her eyes.

"Lift your hair." Cree's breath was warm against her ear, her lips lightly grazing Teresa's earlobe.

She lifted it high and sighed with pleasure when Cree tied the blindfold at the base of her neck, the knot slightly off-center so that it didn't rest against her spine. She let it fall again when Cree turned her around.

"Do you remember the text I sent you after our first date?"

Teresa nodded, loving the feel of the silk against her skin. Unable to see, she thought Cree's voice sounded deeper, smoother, like honey laced with cinnamon. "You said I looked good enough to eat."

"Exactly." Cree kissed her, softly at first, then harder, her tongue slipping into Teresa's mouth. Cree tasted of fine merlot, sultry and smooth. "And do you remember what I told you one of my biggest fantasies is?"

Teresa's breath caught as she thought of the night they'd shared some of their sexual fantasies over a bottle of wine and chocolate-covered cherries. A rush of cool air caressed her skin as she felt Cree unfastening the buttons of her blouse, one by one. "You wanted to watch a group scene."

"Are you willing to be my fantasy?" she whispered as she pulled Teresa's blouse from her shoulders, leaving her standing there in a black lace bra she could feel stretched tight over her hard nipples.

"Group? What, exactly, does that mean?" Teresa felt anxiety begin to build, a knot developing in her stomach. Maybe she'd been wrong to trust so soon. Yeah, the thought was hot, but it was too soon, and in a restaurant full of people?

"Not sex. Relax." Cree's hot mouth traced a line of heated kisses over her shoulder and collar bone to her other shoulder. "Believe me, I want this beautiful body to myself in that way." She bit Teresa's earlobe. "I said you were good enough to eat. I want to show you it's true. Bear with me and I'll show you how good you can feel."

Teresa melted against Cree's hard body, the feel of her strong arms wrapped tightly around her and her mouth pressed to her neck making her weak-kneed. "In that case, make me your fantasy."

Cree moved quickly, stripping Teresa down until she was completely naked. The thought occurred to her briefly that she was glad she'd shaved so her body was smooth. Cree pulled her close, and the feel of her rough clothes against her own nude skin made her feel vulnerable, and incredibly turned on.

"Follow my lead." Cree took her hand and led her across the room.

The wood floor was cool and smooth under her feet, the edge of a pillow soft against the length of her foot.

"Sit down."

She felt the cold edge of the table against her calves and sat, the feeling of polished wood strange against her bare bottom. Cree lifted her legs so she was fully on the table, her big, rough hands wrapped around Teresa's ankles. "Now lie down."

She did so, moving slowly, everything surreal as she lay naked on a table in a restaurant full of people just a hallway away. She could hear the clatter of silverware and glass, the ebb and flow of conversation. Cree's hands slid from her feet up her calves, over her thighs, and the background noise flowed away as she concentrated on the feel of Cree's touch. She stayed away from Teresa's aching center, even though she raised her hips to gain more contact. When she circled Teresa's breasts, squeezing them before pinching the nipples into hard nubs, she nearly came off the table in an effort to keep Cree's touch.

"No, baby. You're going to have to stay very, very still. No matter what you feel, you need to hold still until the end. I promise it will be worth the self-control."

Teresa returned Cree's passionate kiss, excited beyond belief. "You won't leave the room, will you? You'll be here the whole time?"

"I promise. I wouldn't miss it for anything. Now lie still. It's time." Cree pulled her hair out from under her back and let it hang over the edge of the table, and she liked the feel of it swinging free.

Teresa tensed, her senses extra sharp with the loss of her sight. The table stuck to her back and ass, but it wasn't unpleasant. The air was just warm enough to be comfortable without clothing on, not that she imagined anyone else sitting starkers. Low laughter and conversation began filtering into the room, the rustle of material a background symphony. Heels and heavier shoes sounded on the hard floor, and when they got near the table she heard the soft *woosh* of the pillows as the guests sat down around her. Naked, surrounded by strangers, laid out for their gaze, Teresa suddenly wondered what the hell she was doing. Just as she was starting to seriously reconsider, Cree whispered in her ear.

"Ready, baby? Remember not to move."

Knowing Cree was right there next to her helped calm her nerves. She settled into the feeling of being watched, of having a group of women ringed around her, even though she couldn't see them. It appealed to something deep in her psyche and she knew her nipples were hard again. An ice cold, round dish of some kind was placed on her stomach, quickly followed by three more, creating a line from her sternum to her belly button. A longer dish was set down below her belly button, lengthwise, and its base was a bit warmer. The scent of chocolate, warm and heavy, flooded her senses, along with the tang of mint and subtlety of vanilla.

More bowls were balanced carefully along her legs, and the scents of cinnamon, nutmeg and fresh pastry filled the air. Another small bowl was set just below her left shoulder and she was assaulted by the fresh citrus aroma of oranges. Another, on the right shoulder, added the sickly sweet scent of candied cherries. From the space just below her collarbone came the earthy scent of nuts. Her arms were gently manoeuvred so that her palms were up, and pieces of something were placed in each. She wiggled her fingers slightly, trying to get a sense of what it was. In her right hand the pieces were smooth, round. M&Ms, maybe? And in her left hand the pieces were irregular, a round part with a pointed tip. She realized they were probably chocolate chips.

The sound of compressed air was suddenly followed by intense cold, right on top of each nipple at the same time. It took every ounce of control not to jerk, but as the weight of the whipped cream settled past her nipples and began to cover her breasts, the sensation was gorgeous, like sensually spreading icy silk. She nearly moaned at the sensation, and then at the combination of sensations all the way along her body. But she stayed quiet, because tables didn't talk, did they?

There was a moment of silence, and in that moment, she understood exactly what Cree meant by "good enough to eat." She'd been made into some kind of massive dessert bar. She heard someone invite the guests to serve themselves, and the sound of silverware touching ceramic filled the room. She felt each bowl press against her skin as someone dove into its contents. There was something so intense, so primal, about being a giant serving dish. She knew she was wet, and was glad she was blindfolded so no one could see her embarrassment. When the edge of a spoon caught her nipple she couldn't stop a soft moan from escaping, which seemed to inspire the diner to scrape a bit more cream from her achingly hard nipple, the cold metal sliding smoothly over her breast.

It seemed to take forever. The bowls felt like a part of her, and knowing people were eating off her naked body was more erotic than anything she'd ever experienced. The more time passed, the more fluid she felt on her skin. Things dripped from bowls or dribbled from spoons, and she felt a slow, steady slide of a thick, gooey liquid moving down her waist on one side. On the other, something thinner, less viscous, rolled swiftly over her waist and under her back. She felt the whipped cream slipping from her breasts, pooling between them, running down the sides and onto the table beneath her. The enticing individual scents combined to make an overly sweet incense. Eventually the bowls were all lighter, emptied of their contents. Her breasts felt cool and sticky, the nipples hardened by sugar.

The bowls were removed one by one, and her body felt indescribably light, as though she could float right off the table. If she didn't feel somewhat stuck to it, anyway. A pair of hands cupped her face and Cree whispered in her ear, "You're so fucking beautiful. You have no idea how hot that was. Almost as hot as what's about to happen. Remember, hold very still."

She slid the blindfold from Teresa's eyes and she took a moment to adjust to the dim light. Being able to see the group of women seated around her made her wish the blindfold was back in place. But a quick glance around them assured her she needn't worry about it. To them she was a curvy table, something unusual, and not much more. They were barely looking at her. At least, that's what she told herself. Cree knelt down next to her and plucked at Teresa's nipple, making her jump slightly. Someone chuckled, but she continued to look at Cree. She saw fire reflected in Cree's eyes and looked beyond her, at the door.

Flames flickered and sparked, sending dancing shadows over the diners and walls, creating a wicked atmosphere, something hedonistic and sexy. Plenty of hushed *oohs* and *ahhs* sounded as the Flaming Baked Alaska was brought in on a heavy ceramic plate. Teresa held still as it was placed on her stomach, the bottom hot but not uncomfortably so. The flames sent shadows over her body, highlighting the curves and valleys covered in sweet, sticky sauces. It burned itself out and the waiters went to work, drizzling hot fudge from her neck to her toes, long swirls of hot, thick chocolate sauce.

Small bowls of large, fire-engine red strawberries were placed in front of the diners, and they quickly dove in. They carved out pieces of the Alaska for themselves, and dipped their strawberries in the chocolate covering her body, their hands everywhere. Leaning, pressing, scooping up bits of chocolate from her skin and licking it off their fingers. Teresa closed her eyes and revelled in the feel of so many hands on every part of her body except the one place where she needed them most. She felt her wetness flow, dripping down to puddle beneath her.

She watched as Cree swirled a strawberry in the fudge over her nipples, making her moan once again. "Open up, beautiful." Teresa opened her mouth, sucking at the tart chocolate and keeping her eyes locked on Cree. "I can't wait to get you alone," she murmured, watching Teresa suck the fruit into her mouth.

She moved away to chat with someone, and Teresa relaxed. The number of hands on her skin had decreased, leaving her warm, sticky, sweet, and strangely exhausted. Soon the diners began to leave, and more than one gave Teresa a wink or grin. When the room had emptied, she looked at Cree, sitting sprawled in the chair and watching her. Cree stood, and Teresa was mesmerized at her lupine grace. Right now, she looked like she was stalking prey.

"I didn't have anything to eat. Do you know why?" She stood at the end of the table, near Teresa's feet. "Because I knew I'd be having my dessert later." She knelt and took Teresa's foot in her mouth, slowly sucking each toe before moving up to her ankle. Inch by inch, she licked the various sauces from Teresa's legs until she got to her center. She pressed her tongue to Teresa's clit and sucked hard. She arched from the table, pushing herself into Cree's mouth. She was so hard she knew she wouldn't last long, which was probably why Cree stopped quickly, licking a long line up Teresa's soaking wetness, and then began sucking and nipping at her stomach, until she reached her breasts.

She sucked each nipple in turn, licking them clean, making circles around her breasts as she removed the last vestiges of whipped cream. She bit lightly on her nipples, sucking them in, tugging on them.

"Please. Jesus, Cree, please. You're killing me."

Cree grinned and kissed her deeply, her tongue pressed hard into Teresa's mouth. She tasted like the best ice cream sundae ever made, like ice on a hot summer day, like a fire on a cold night. She was everything all at once, and Teresa wanted more, so much more. She wrapped a hand in Cree's hair, not caring that her palms were sticky. She tugged hard. "Damn it, Cree. Please."

She gasped when Cree obligingly slid two fingers inside her, deep and hard. "Yes. God, yes. More."

Cree added another finger, and then a fourth, filling Teresa completely, while continuing to lick and bite at her nipples and the soft, sticky skin of her pale breasts. She pumped hard and Teresa didn't think it could feel any more perfect, any more amazing, than it did. But then Cree pressed her thumb against Teresa's rock-hard clit and she couldn't hold back anymore. She exploded, driving herself down on Cree's hand, pressing her breast into her mouth. The smell of arousal mixed with the scent of sugar and it was intoxicating in a whole new way.

Cree rested her chin on Teresa's stomach and looked up at her, a cat-canary grin on her face. "So? Was I right? Was it as amazing as it looked?"

Teresa nodded, but could barely keep her eyes open. "Amazing. But why am I so tired?"

Cree was off her and holding up a thick robe in an instant. "Because you had to keep your muscles tensed for hours. That's exhausting. And impressive."

Teresa struggled into the robe and leaned into Cree's embrace. "Take me home, stud, and we'll talk about it there."

Cree led them through a back door to her truck, which was parked close by. When they were on the road, Cree glanced over at her. "Did you enjoy it, really? You seemed to."

Teresa slid her hand up Cree's inner thigh. "Totally incredible. I mean, being an object of sorts like that, it never even occurred to me. But it was so hot to think of those people eating right off my body." She squeezed the soft skin of Cree's thigh. "The question is, how did it make you feel?"

Cree's expression was serious. "You know, at first I actually felt a bit weird. Like, in the first moment I was actually a little jealous of those people touching you. And then I saw how hard your nipples were, and I could see how wet you were. It made me relax, and I just enjoyed watching them eat all that stuff off you. You just looked…fucking beautiful. Amazing."

Teresa's stomach tumbled at the soft, clearly heartfelt admission. In that moment, in a fuzzy robe and covered in drying sugar, she'd never felt as sexy as she did right then.

She undid her seat belt and slid closer so she could nuzzle Cree's neck. "Thank you. Knowing you were there meant I knew I was safe. And it made me hotter knowing you were watching all those women eat me, so to speak."

Cree chuckled as they pulled into the driveway. "Well, we're not quite done. Come on, sugar-tits. Let's get you cleaned up."

She followed Cree into the house and directly to the bathroom. She removed the robe as Cree turned the water on full blast.

"I'll be right back. Hop in and I'll join you in a second." She kissed Teresa gently, so softly, so sweetly, it nearly brought tears to her eyes.

She got in and let the hot water soothe her tense muscles and wash away the vestiges of her experience. The door slid open and Cree stepped in behind her. She pressed her chest to Teresa's back, her small, firm breasts hard against Teresa's shoulder blades, her strong thighs taut against her ass.

"You know, I'm still hungry." Teresa opened her eyes and watched as Cree held a container of honey overhead and tipped it so that a long, thin stream slid over Teresa's breasts. She moaned and rested her head against Cree's shoulder as the honey trickled down her stomach and onto her thighs, mixing with the hot water and steam so that she felt like she was encased in a honeypot. Cree turned her around and their bodies slid together, slick and wet. She poured out a handful of honey and set the container aside. With her free hand, she moved Teresa so that her back was pressed against the cool shower tiles and she cupped Teresa's hot, wet center, just barely grazing it, with the handful of honey before she rubbed the honey into both hands and then spread it over Teresa's thighs, massaging it in, all the way down her calves.

She rested on her knees and kept Teresa's gaze as she lowered her mouth to her and sucked on her clit before sliding her tongue through her folds. Her honeyed hands grasped Teresa's ass and held her still as she sucked and licked Teresa into a frenzy of wordless pleading. When Teresa felt like she was going to explode, Cree stopped and slowly stood, so that every inch of her came into contact with Teresa's body until she was fully pressed against her, both of them covered in warm sweetness. She hoisted Teresa and lifted her legs so they were wrapped around her waist and kissed her deeply. Wet, warm honey coated Teresa's mouth and she sucked it greedily from Cree's tongue, stopping only when Cree pressed three fingers deep and hard inside her and began fucking her hard, just the way she needed. She held onto Cree's shoulders and rode her hand.

"Please. Cree, please—I'm going to..."

Cree thrust harder and faster. "Let go."

She did, coming harder than she could ever remember coming in her life, Cree's moan of pleasure driving her even further over the edge.

They stayed that way, pressed against the tile, honeyed steam filling the bathroom and stroking their bodies, until they both caught their breath. Cree slowly let Teresa's legs down and caressed her face. "You okay?"

Teresa kissed her, and tried to put every ounce of the sensual, sublime feeling she had coursing through her into it. Cree's eyes closed and she whispered, "Guess so."

They showered off quietly, lost in the haze of sexual afterglow. Cree washed Teresa's backside thoroughly, making her gasp when she washed her sensitive bit quite thoroughly. They got out and Cree cloaked her in a thick, soft towel.

Her skin felt alive, heightened by the experience of so many textures, smells, and tastes.

Cree wrapped her in a tight hug. "What say we go to bed? I've got plans for our breakfast tomorrow."

Teresa grinned. "Am I breakfast?"

"Maybe. If you're lucky."

DESSERT PLATTER

Ingredients

Various fruits, cut up

Whipped Cream

Warm Chocolate Sauce

Beautiful naked woman, optional

Directions

Dip the fruit into the whipped cream and warm chocolate sauce, both spread out luxuriously over the beautiful naked woman. Alternatively, you can use a serving dish.

Enjoy!

APPETIZING

CHERI CRYSTAL

Editorial Note: In Cheri's story, "appetizing" is used as a noun, as well as an adjective, referring to a specific section of a deli counter. This is a term specific to New York City and is unknown outside of the city's Metro area. It arose to accommodate Jewish dietary law, which mandates that meats be separated from fish and dairy. Meats are purchased at the deli, fish and dairy at the appetizing counter.

AFTER A BLUSTERY WINTER, SPRING is a welcome mood raiser. The days are lengthening and it's still light at 6:15 when I park at the shopping center and head inside. I zip around the supermarket, loading my cart, hoping to make it home before sunset to cut the grass after a quick bite to eat. The numbers flash, indicating that my turn at the deli and appetizing counter is getting closer.

Too busy caring for an ornery, but admirable, WWII veteran nurse for eleven hours, I haven't eaten much all day. I work my way to the display case and my taste buds awaken in response to the enticing smell of sour pickles in huge barrels. They tempt me into buying delicatessen instead of appetizing. Dinner plans change from a bagel, cream cheese, and lox to pastrami on rye in a matter of seconds. The thought of cold cuts with a side order of coleslaw and a pickle makes my stomach growl loud enough to be heard without a microphone. I place a jar of Hebrew National deli mustard in my cart, help myself to a pint of half-sour pickles, and scribble rye bread on my list. My mouth waters. I'm chomping at the bit to take a bite.

I'm ready to order one of every available item when I hear: "Now serving number sixty-nine."

My arm automatically shoots up, I almost shout, "Bingo," but don't, and when I glance toward my server, it's as if I have just swallowed a hot dog whole.

I swear, I do not fall in lust easily. So, imagine my surprise when I instantly go from starving for food to hungering for the incredible sight before my eyes. She is truly scrumptious in a pretty, perky, yet sturdy, sort of way. Her smile says it all. If the lights suddenly blew, she would be the torch.

She clears her throat. I'm caught staring and turn redder than the brightest roasted pepper—make that a hot, spicy roasted pepper. I'm on fire.

The moment my brain cells rejuvenate, I long to ask this curvaceous goddess where she has been all my life, but don't dare. She reminds me of the pin-up-girl/woman-at-work images on the Internet. It's no mystery why these photographs were used during WWII to keep GI morale high. Lucky for me this beauty is living and breathing in the twenty-first century or I would have been born in the wrong era.

I step up, flash a friendly smile, and freeze as she peers back at me until she ultimately asks, "What can I get you tonight, gorgeous?"

I relax in response to her cheery disposition and have a bunch of good answers to her questions, but instead I reply, "I'll have four slices of the kosher pastrami that's on sale, please." Kosher deli brings me back to my childhood spent sharing meals in Brooklyn before we all moved out to Long Island with the entire *mishpuchah*. Ours was a huge extended family and we sure enjoyed our food. This robust girl would fit right in.

"Good choice, but only four slices? Are you sure you don't want half a pound?"

"No, thanks, I'll come by tomorrow and buy more," I say, dropping a hint and hoping she'll be my server again.

She takes the Empire Kosher turkey pastrami and places it on the slicer. She is so cool. Her skin is like pure silk, tinted with a subtle tan. I worry about her lovely fingers so close to the sharp blade, but I'm soon reassured by her prowess around a power tool.

While she works, I assess her attributes, notably her generous behind, well-defined curves, and strong arms and shoulders. Decked out in full uniform, any other woman would appear all washed out wearing white from head to toe, but she possesses a vibrant aura that entices, captivates, and ignites the senses. She is more gorgeous than I am, but I gladly accept her compliment.

I glance at her nametag. "Jacklyn," it says, but my sight automatically focuses on her ample breasts. I long to get my hands and mouth around them. She places the package, neatly wrapped in wax paper and cellophane, on the counter. I'm seriously trying not to gawk and quickly look up. It's no hardship, since I'm mesmerized by her eyes. They are liquid brown with hints of hazel and specks of gold. Her hair is slicked back beneath one of the white paper hats all the workers wear for sanitary reasons, but a few strands fall free to brush her forehead despite the hat.

"What else can I get you?" She's obviously checking me out and she smiles.

I want to ask for her phone number for starters, but my words get stuck. I'm even tempted to ask for a generous helping of tongue, to gauge her reaction, but my bravado has gone AWOL. I finally manage to say, "I'll have two slices of your sharpest cheddar, please."

I hold myself up by resting my hand on the counter. After she fills my order, the heat from her touch as she hands me the cheese registers as she places her hand on top of mine. I jump.

"Sorry. I didn't mean to startle you," she says, but she appears more amused than apologetic.

"I was just thinking..." My words disappear as I reach out for what she's offering, our fingers touch again, linger. We're practically in a trance, until we're rudely interrupted by a gruff old gent who wants to know how long until it's his turn.

"It won't be long, sir," she assures him. Returning her attention, she gives me a wink, and I nearly melt. She leans in closer. "The chicken soup is worth a try. Not to brag, but I made the matzo balls from scratch. Would you like to try some?"

"Sure, I'll take a quart with extra matzo balls." If hers are half as good as Grandma's, I'll have to marry her.

She hands me the plastic container. "Can I get you anything else?" There's that teasing, suggestive tone again. I'm ready to leap over the counter and gobble her up.

A kiss would be nice. "No, thank you. I'm good. For now."

"See you tomorrow, then."

I'm speechless. She's written her phone number on the package of pastrami using a black marker. I race through the aisles, absently grabbing stuff off the shelves, until I'm swiping my credit card at the register without a thought to what I've purchased or how much I've spent. No sooner have the automatic doors swung open and I exit the store, I spot her sitting on the benches by the recycling center with her back to me. Her hat is off and every hair is perfectly feathered in back, like a well-preened duck's tail, and wild with varying warm shades of red, burgundy, orange, and gold. Such eclectic highlights complement her chestnut roots and olive skin tone. I'm tempted to go over. I know she's interested, otherwise she wouldn't have flirted shamelessly, recommended her soup, or given me her phone number. I am usually much bolder than this, but my mind and stomach flip-flop. Should I or shouldn't I?

I wheel my cart in her direction, elated that she seems to want to see me again. Just as I get closer, she and two of the checkout girls take off for the employees' entrance. In the wake of a missed opportunity, I have no choice but to get in my car and go home. I heat up her chicken soup and drool all over myself with how light and fluffy her matzo balls are. Then I fry up the pastrami to have on rye with mustard, coleslaw, and a half-sour pickle. I wash it down with Dr. Brown's Cream Soda and envision sharing this blast from the past—eating at the Canarsie Kosher Deli—with her as I decide when to call.

To avoid appearing anxious, I should probably wait three days, but instead, I wait three hours, and pray that

10:30 p.m. isn't too late. She answers on the first ring. My heart rate soars, as do my hopes.

"Hi, it's Reba. Is Jacklyn there?" I ask, just to be sure she doesn't have a twin, not that a clone would be a bad thing.

"Well, hello, gorgeous. This is she. Reba? Nice name. It suits you, actually. Do you know what Reba means?"

She's not shy and she's easy to talk to. "No clue, but I'm sure you'll fill me in."

"Oh, I'll fill you in any way you want…" Her voice trails off and I get lost in wishful thinking when I hear her fingers tapping a keyboard. I can imagine what other gifts her fingertips possess. She is quiet for a moment, before she states, "Reba means 'to tie, bind, trap, and snare'." She chuckles. "It just so happens that that is exactly what I have in mind for you. What do you say?"

"Yes!" I don't have to think about it. At this point I will take whatever she has to offer.

"Excellent. You mentioned you'll be by the store tomorrow. If you don't mind shopping around until I get off, you can come home with me afterwards. I have a catering gig on Sunday, a rich client with lots of friends I'm trying to impress, and I need a guinea pig to try out some of my new recipes. You interested?"

"Sure, I'm game," I say without a moment's hesitation, even though I don't know anything about her besides her name, where she works, and that she's possibly into bondage. Tasting her food will be way more than icing on the cake, if her matzo balls are any indication of her talent.

"Perfect." She sounds pleased.

"What would you like me to bring?"

"Just yourself, a hearty appetite, and an open mind. We can get everything else we need before we leave the supermarket. Dinner is on me."

"I live a few miles from the supermarket," she tells me. "Sounds great."

"I'm thirty, I live alone, I'm squeaky clean, and I love food and sex, and not necessarily in that order. Now tell me more about you."

I take a deep breath and just dive in. "I'm thirty-four, I live alone, I'm also squeaky clean, and I adore food and sex. You can cook and I can eat, so I would say we're a match made in heaven."

We chat for hours. I love talking to her and hate to hang up but it's four in the morning and we both have work in a few hours. I tell her I'm a home healthcare aide for an elderly woman named Florence who needs reminding that she's no longer an Army nurse and WWII is long since over. I assure Jacklyn that Florence's last name begins with a "C" and not "N" as in Nightingale. I am sharing stories about how the Jaws of Life aren't strong enough to pry Florence's lips open when she refuses to eat, until Jacklyn is laughing so hard she confides she's nearly peed herself.

After we manage to hang up, there's a huge smile on my face the size of an endless buffet. I'm so high on life, I can't sleep. I'm already planning what wine to bring and which flowers to cut from my garden, deciding that the daffodils and tulips are vibrant at the moment and would be a nice touch.

Unable to pick a wine, I choose a bottle of white and a bottle of red from the top shelf of my wine rack, which I save for special occasions. I'm merrily humming Billy Joel's "Scenes From An Italian Restaurant," as I put the white in the fridge to chill while I get ready for work. I pack a change of clothes, filling a knapsack with a pair of form-fitted Levi's and a snug knit top. I throw in my sexiest bra and matching panties, soap bag because she's promised me a shower and Jacuzzi the moment we get to her house, and assemble a homemade bouquet, adding a few sprigs of forsythia because I don't grow baby's breath.

As an afterthought, I take along a toothbrush and paste, just in case. I'm clearly getting ahead of myself, but I can't help it and don't care to.

A shower clears my head. Naked, I towel off and check for spots I missed with the razor. Not finding any, I'm pleased that I've managed to maintain some semblance of the musculature I worked hard to keep by gardening and lifting Florence in and out of a chair. My arms and thighs don't show the signs of aging and my abs, while not a six-pack by any stretch of the imagination, are not too shabby either. My breasts are not a worry—they're average-sized, they don't sag too badly, and the nipple rings really add to their sensitivity.

The bane of my appearance is my ultra-fine hair. I keep it short and use enough products to stock a hair salon, or it would go totally limp in seconds. I hope it holds. I want to be all gussied up so she'll want to rip my clothes off. I get a pleasant ache below and hope that my clit won't be neglected tonight.

All day at work, Florence is uncharacteristically cooperative. "What's gotten into you?" I ask, after she complies with my requests the first time I ask.

"If you were glowing any brighter you'd burn out my cataracts! Who is the lucky woman?"

"Say what?" I'm dumbfounded. We don't usually discuss this sort of thing.

"Oh, come on, now. I wasn't born yesterday. Far from it. I can smell a hot-to-trot woman from a mile away."

"Well, if you must know, I have a date tonight and she's beautiful. She can cook, too."

"Go get her, Tiger. And I want the juicy details on Monday, or else."

I dub Florence, who I call Mrs. C because she deserves respect, the coolest lady of her entire generation. She's lived through World War II and doesn't have qualms about my sexual preference, and it's a refreshing change to be around someone who is above petty prejudices.

When my shift is done, Florence calls me over. "Reba, go and fetch my vase out of the china cabinet. The one on the top shelf."

I do as she asks. "Now go rinse it out for the flowers you brought. And please do an old woman a favor and dispose of the tacky tin foil."

"I'm sorry, Mrs. C, but the flowers are for my date."

"I know, I know, and they should have a proper vase."

She doesn't take no for an answer. The vase isn't a family heirloom, but still, her generosity warms me to my toes. I give her a hug and she pats my cheek in return. "Anyone worth the air they breathe would be very lucky to have you. Good luck tonight."

I am all choked up, and thankful for a job I like, but TGIF!

A few minutes after 6:00, I arrive at the deli counter and watch as Jacklyn serves customers. She makes small talk and has them laughing like they're old friends. I could watch her all day but I really need to put my tongue back in my mouth again.

She flashes me a smile and hands me a sheet of paper. "I hope you don't mind gathering these items while I finish up here. Just promise you won't go to checkout before I do. Promise?"

"Promise." I glance down at the list and just know I'm going to be in for the gastronomic treat of a lifetime. I've never bought a shallot or baked a chocolate molten lava cake in my life.

"Any questions?"

"How do you know I'll choose the right ones?"

"I trust you. Besides, I can check your work in an hour. That's how long you have. Concentrate on quality—do *not* check price. I have it covered. Are you up for it?"

"You know I am."

"Good, now go."

I'm an ordinary cook—roast chicken, baked fish, broiled steaks and potatoes, steamed veggies, salads, lasagna maybe, are more my speed. I hate to admit to relying heavily on convenience items like jarred marinara sauce, but it's the truth. There are some really good frozen dinners out there, and, of course, sandwiches, pasta, and omelettes are quick and easy in a pinch.

She has so many ingredients on the list, my head spins. I wonder if she's a master chef in disguise with meticulous handwriting to match.

My lust quotient and appetite soar as I imagine her capable hands at work and other hidden talents I hope to discover. Her hands should be insured.

I look over the menu:

Herbed Tomato Bread
Garlic Butter

126

Chicken Liver Pate
Oysters Rockefeller
Filet Mignon Cabernet
Potatoes au Gratin with Caramelized Shallots
Asparagus
Chocolate Molten Lava Cake à la mode

And then at the shopping list:

Chicken livers, Filet Mignon and bacon (from butcher
holding my package in the back, ring buzzer)
Oysters (ordered special by fishmonger)
2 lemons
1 bunch fresh asparagus
1 head curly lettuce
1 bag fresh spinach
3 large Vidalia onions
2 shallots
1 pound sweet butter
1 quart heavy cream
Ice cream (the richer, the better, choose favorite to go
with chocolate molten lava cake)

My gastronomic, and other juices, are flowing readily.
Does she know the aphrodisiacal powers of oysters?

Once I finish collecting the items on her list, I head back
to the appetizing counter just in time.

"Let's check what you have here," Jacklyn says, surveying the chosen goods.

I hold my breath.

"You've done a fine job, Reba."

"Thank you."

"Let me pay and we're off."

"Are you sure I can't at least chip in?"

"Absolutely not. You're doing me a favor. Besides—" she says with a wink, "maybe we can take it out in trade."

"That sounds like a great plan to me. Let's not linger here."

"I like your attitude. I hope you're hungry."

"Starving." And for more than just food.

I follow her Mini Cooper, blue with wide white stripes, to a development I've actually been to a million times before. In fact, my aunt and uncle used to live nearby before they retired to Florida. Who knew I'd meet a girl from this quaint part of town? I'm flooded with fond memories of running around with my cousins, riding bikes and getting into all sorts of mischief on these very streets. It's comforting to be back.

She parks in a widened driveway and waves me on to park my car beside hers. There's ample room for the prized Beetle I bought off my brother. I am into cars almost as much as I'm into food, but there's no contest—sex tops my list. I'm far from promiscuous—she has to be special—and so far, I haven't found her. Until now.

"Love your car," I say, as she pops the trunk.

"Same here. What year?"

"It's a '74."

"Sweet."

"Speaking of sweet, your menu has me salivating enough to fill Oyster Bay."

"That's what I like to hear. I'll grab some groceries."

"I'll help."

"Thanks. Follow me."

Her modest home is clean, bright, and cozy with scents of freshly picked lilacs. The entrance hall is only big enough for a half-moon rug with space to remove our shoes and leads into a traditional living room decorated in Early American with Laura Ashley-type furnishings. The wall-mounted television, opposite a Lazy Boy and overstuffed sofa, is the only item that hints at contemporary.

Farther along is the country kitchen with counter space and cabinets that go on for miles. Well, not quite miles, but at first glance, a huge chunk of change was obviously invested in the kitchen. I would be hard-pressed to name an appliance or amenity it may be lacking. The spice rack, with its array of fresh herbs and spices, and cooking utensils alone are impressive. She's not kidding when she claims to be into catering. If her sexual appetite is anything like her passion for food, I am going to be the happiest woman on Earth, and possibly in the entire universe.

"Make yourself at home and I'll give you the tour. Then we can get started."

"I will, but first I need to go out to my car a minute."

"Sure, leave the front door open. I'll begin here and then we can have drinks, get washed up, or whatever your heart desires."

I run out to the car, throw my knapsack over one shoulder to have two hands free to grab the gifts. I should have purchased a proper vase, but I'm grateful to Mrs. C and her comment about tin foil being tacky. The old gal is one smart cookie.

Once inside again, I remove my shoes and close the door. There's lots of activity going on in the kitchen. I hear the convection motor running until she opens the oven door and the noise stops briefly. I watch as she puts a risen loaf of red-tinted bread on the rack and shuts the door. The fan's hum and the rattling of pans on top of the stove resume.

"This will take a while to bake. I prepared it before work."

I hand her the bottles of wine and place the vase on the table. Then I give her the flowers I have tucked under my arm.

"You shouldn't have, but these are lovely. And wine, too? You went overboard."

"Not really. The flowers are from my garden and I collect wine for special occasions."

She beams and my heart melts.

I help her fill the vase. She sniffs the flowers, adds a few of her lilacs, and we admire the bouquet as she places it in the center of an elegantly set table. She puts the white in the fridge to keep it cool. "Just in case, but this red is rich. An ideal accompaniment for filet mignon. Thank you very much." I'm relieved to have brought both, especially the Chilean Cabernet Sauvignon. It's one of my favorites.

"Now that the bread is baking, I'll pan-fry the filets just before we eat them, and may even let you help me mix up a mean molten cake—the creamy center oozes out like liquid chocolate lava—you'll love it." What an understatement.

"Let me show you around. You can freshen up while I cook. Okay if I take a quick shower first?"

"Of course." At this point I am wondering what her bondage comment was all about, but to be honest, I'm so happy with this pace that I haven't a smidgen of complaint.

It's a breeze not to feel like I have to perform right from the start. This never happens to me.

I prefer to wait for a drink, and we go up the long staircase to the bedrooms and main bathroom. The master bedroom is on the right, and she gives me a quick peek. Like the rest of the house, it's traditional, with a floral-patterned bedspread and matching window treatments. There is a potpourri of scents I can only describe as fresh and crisp, like white linen sheets. To the left of the bathroom is another bedroom. The furniture is totally funky and functional like an Ikea showroom. There's a full-sized bed, night table, wardrobe, love seat, console TV, bookshelves filled with cookbooks, and a desktop computer.

"This is the guest bedroom. You can put your stuff in here. Would you like to watch TV or use the computer while I change?"

I'm mildly disappointed, but truly relieved when she doesn't offer a shower for two because the longer she delays satisfying my hunger, the better it will be when I finally eat. The luscious scent of homemade bread wafts upstairs and hits me hard. I can eat a horse.

Not long after, I look up from the TV, without a clue which channel is on, when she enters in only a towel covering the important parts. I nearly fall off the couch.

"That was quick," I say, biting my bottom lip to keep my tongue in my mouth.

She hands me a fluffy towel. "Next. And feel free to take your time. Have a Jacuzzi if you like."

"I'd like a Jacuzzi, but only if you join me."

"That can be arranged at some point, but if I don't feed you first, you'll faint before I have my way with you."

"If your wishes are anything like mine, then we're both going to need plenty of fuel."

"I knew I liked you the moment you walked over to my counter. Enjoy your shower."

"Thank you." I carry my soap bag and change of clothes to the bathroom and strip. It is ultra-modern, smartly done, and I can see my nude body from every single angle. I blush, although I'm alone. I could easily fuck her in here, but first things first. I know what she is whipping up in the kitchen and I am dying to partake.

Barefoot, in my jeans and top, I join her in the kitchen, chock-full of delicious aromas. The table is set with fine china, candles, and stemware, which, she explains, were her Granny's. The elegance isn't lost on me and I wonder how she can afford this feast on a supermarket salary. She is wearing a silk shirt, pleated trousers, and pumps. The apron is all that protects her outfit, yet she's spotless. She's obviously cooked in this garb before. I wonder if I'm dressed all right, but she soon puts my mind at ease, with a tender kiss on the lips.

"You look good enough to eat," she states. Then she nips my bottom lip and I'm weak in the knees. "While the cabernet breathes, mind opening the Pinot Grigio you brought?"

"Sure thing, gorgeous."

"Uh-uh-uh, that's my pet name for you. You'll have to come up with something original."

"Truly scrumptious."

She laughs. That's from *Chitty Chitty Bang Bang*, and not very original."

"True, but it suits you. Okay, I'll call you 'appetizing' because you're the most appetizing woman I've ever met."

"Aw, that's sweet. Pour the wine, gorgeous, and I'll join you momentarily." She has four types of glasses on the table.

How does she know where everything goes? There are so many forks, knives, and spoons, I thank God I had a teacher who was into etiquette or I wouldn't know where to start.

"I hope you're ready for this," she says, interrupting my thoughts.

"I was born ready. Bring it on, baby."

She places a basket of sliced tomato bread on the table with home-churned butter she's infused with garlic and a few secret ingredients.

The bread is still warm. Crispy crust, chewy texture inside, hints of tomato and basil. The butter melts with flavors that burst on my palate and tickle my tongue.

"O-M-F-G, this is unbelievable!"

"I take it you like it then?" She dabs at the corner of my mouth where butter has collected.

"I could eat the whole loaf, but I'll be polite and leave you some."

"Very considerate of you."

I love her sexy smile. We toast to us and many more dinners to come.

Next, she places liver pâté, crackers, and dots of assorted sauces on my plate. Its smooth, tasty goodness goes down easily. I'm trying not to inhale my food, but it's delicious. I say as much, but she tells me to *shush* and just savor it.

Not to mention what the oysters, reminiscent of the delicate parts of a woman, do to me. We exchange twin looks with salacious intent.

"I am so horny," I blurt. "Would it be okay if we take a break before the main course?"

"I was so hoping, praying, you would say that. The main course can wait."

I stand up. The linen napkin falls off my lap and hers does, too. The next thing I know, we're making out like bandits, stealing gropes and kisses. Her lips are soft and succulent. My mind spins with overwhelming desire—the food and wine have gone to my head.

"Reba, where have you been all my life?" She's breathless.

"I was wondering the same about you."

"Let's go. Bedroom. Quick."

"I want to fuck you in every room of the house."

"That can be arranged."

We hurry, stripping and dropping clothes, until we're streaking through her house. I follow her up the stairs—her butt is the carrot and I am the ravenous hare in heat chasing close behind. Her body glistens, fragrant lust fills the air, beckoning me until I can barely stand still. She throws off the decorative pillows and comforter and we fall onto her bed, both wet with want and locked in a heated embrace.

She grasps my head in her hands, tangling her fingers through my hair, to pull me close. I kiss her silken skin, trying not to miss any.

She then guides me onto my back.

She's on top, her hand cups my crotch, a finger glides through my silken folds, and my clit swells beneath her fingertips. I gasp. Toying with my damp mound, she brings me ever closer and urgent for release. I distract myself by pulling her in by her waist, bringing her breasts toward my lips, suckling one nipple, careful not to neglect the other, amidst dual moans of pleasure. She groans as I knead her breasts, so I pinch her nipples to pleasurable points.

She ravishes my lips, my breasts, and runs her tongue along my belly until she reaches the apex between my thighs. "This," she says, "I'm saving for dessert."

I groan and she flops onto her back. I'm tempted to tickle-torture her, but when she spreads her legs, revealing her precious oyster, I'm ready. I move in to take her. Her clit enlarges under my thumb, her pussy welcomes my fingers. It's easy to get lost inside her—I don't ever want to be found. I pump her at a rate that mirrors her grinding hips. She fucks me with her thigh as if we've sampled this menu a million times before. Our momentous cries of rapture mingle. We come together, before we go limp. I'm sated, yet hungry for more.

"That was delicious," she says. "I think I'm ready for the main course now. You?"

"Absolutely. Where's the beef?"

She giggles. "In the kitchen. Come help me test the rest of the menu, and let's make love in every room of the house while we're at it. How does that sound?"

"Appetizing."

HOT PASTRAMI ON RYE

Ingredients

3 to 6 oz. lean kosher pastrami from your favorite deli

1 to 2 schmears margarine (pareve for those who keep kosher)

2 to 4 slices of seedless Jewish rye bread

1 to 2 teaspoons Hebrew National Deli Mustard

¼ cup coleslaw

1 sour or half-sour pickle, cut in wedges, as garnish

Directions

1. In a lightly greased fry pan (use cooking spray, vegetable oil, or margarine), heat up pastrami over medium heat for about 2-3 minutes on both sides. Pastrami is already cooked so it just needs to be heated.

2. Add a thin schmear of margarine (margarine for kosher; butter, if preferred) to both sides of the bread and mustard on the inside (the amount, to taste.) Make a sandwich with the pastrami and mustard on the inside and the buttered sides on the outside. You can make one overstuffed sandwich using all the pastrami and only two slices of rye or make two smaller ones with 3 oz. pastrami in each, depending on your appetite. Kosher delis typically overstuff their sandwiches—it's an unwritten law, I think.

3. Next, fry or grill the sandwich, much like you would a grilled cheese, so that both sides are cooked to a lovely golden brown with the bread toasted but not burnt.

4. Serve this scrumptious hot pastrami sandwich immediately and enjoy it with a side order of coleslaw and a crisp and succulent sour or half-sour pickle. Pickles are fine out of a jar, but pickles right out of the barrel truly rock. Have a glass of seltzer with ice and lemon—my beverage of choice—or a Dr. Brown's Cream Soda as a great accompaniment. My mouth waters just typing this. Enjoy.

SUGAR AND 'SHINE

ANDI MARQUETTE

SUNNY FINISHED CLEANING THE PAINTBRUSH she'd been using to cut along the baseboard and window frames in the living room. She wrapped the sodden roller head in a plastic bag and covered the paint can before she stepped back and appraised her work. The off-white really brightened the room, especially since Jimmy had refinished all the dark wood floors. Behind her, the front door stood open to the covered front porch of the bungalow to help alleviate the paint fumes. The floor fan she'd set up nearby didn't really cool the air, but it at least gave her an illusion of that.

Funny, how a place she'd grown up in could feel so different. The only furniture in it now was a card table and two lawn chairs in the dining room and a futon couch in the bedroom she was using upstairs, which had actually been her bedroom when she was a kid. Jimmy's makeover with floors, lighting, and paint made it feel like somebody else's house. Which it would be, soon enough. They both wanted it on the market in another month. He'd finish the HVAC tomorrow, so she had another night sleeping next to the old window unit, but she didn't mind. She'd dealt with worse.

She pulled the bandanna from the back pocket of her shorts and wiped the sweat off her face then decided she might as well get a quick shower. Afterward, feeling much better in clean shorts and a tank, she went into the kitchen. Leftover pizza and a bottle of Coke in the fridge had "dinner" written all over them. She took the Coke out and drank some of it.

She took the pizza out and hesitated before she closed the fridge, the big glass jug on the bottom shelf bringing back a swirl of memories. It was almost full, and Sunny knew it wasn't Daddy's moonshine—the last batch he'd made before he died a year ago went to his neighborhood friends—but it still made her think about him, and how he'd shown both her and Jimmy his recipe when they were growing up. Mama never complained about it, since it kept him home rather than out at the bars drinking after his shifts at the plant. In a weird way, helping him with a batch was a bonding experience between Sunny, Jimmy, and him.

Daddy could make anything and fix anything. Moonshine was one of his talents, and he'd gotten the recipe from his daddy, who got it from his daddy before that. All the way back to the boat, he'd liked to joke, but Sunny figured it probably wasn't a joke. And now Jimmy continued the family tradition, right down to keeping it chilled. She closed the fridge and ate two pieces of pizza cold and chugged the rest of the Coke. On a whim, she searched the brand new kitchen cabinets that Jimmy had installed, and smiled when she found it. An empty Mason jar, probably left over from Daddy's last batch. He probably knew she and Jimmy pilfered 'shine for fun back in high school, but he never said anything, only told them that if they ever got in trouble to call him.

She took the jug out and poured the Mason jar half-full, kicked her flip-flops off, and went out onto the front porch, where Jimmy had replaced the swing with a newer model. She sat down and stared past the big magnolia that shaded the front of the house to the street, and she remembered all the summers she'd spent tearing around the block with some of the neighbor kids. Wasn't a yard that could keep them out, and bedtimes didn't matter because they'd sneak out anyway and play baseball in the warm humid night air until teen hormones kicked in and instead of baseball, they'd meet friends at the Sonic, where they pretended they were bigger and badder than any of them actually were, and they'd sneak peeks at classmates they thought were cute.

Sunny thought about the crushes she'd had on her female classmates and how she had buried those deep, until the night she and Antoinette Robinson shared a jar of Daddy's moonshine after a football game on the edge of town, where the tang of Gulf Coast air mixed with the heavy, rich smell of Alabama cropland. And as harsh as that moonshine tasted in her own mouth, it was honey on Antoinette's lips and it was spicy on her tongue, and Sunny decided that was the shit, there in her daddy's beat-up panel truck, making out with Antoinette Robinson like they were starving for each other's mouths.

But like that moonshine, once it was gone, so was Antoinette, unless she was looking to get past one of her many boyfriend dramas. Sunny obliged, for the most part, because she liked how it felt to hold and taste a woman, and she liked how Antoinette's brown skin contrasted with hers when they fooled around, and how Antoinette would joke that they were a chocolate-vanilla swirl ice cream cone. And then she'd go back to her parents' big house on the rich side of town and make up with her boyfriend a few days later.

Sometimes it hurt, but most times Sunny shrugged it off. Money, culture, and color were intractable lines here, and after high school, everything would change, anyway.

She took her first sip, ready for the familiar taste of Daddy's 'shine, but as it rolled across her tongue, she realized right away that it wasn't Daddy's. It had hints of his recipe, but this was all Jimmy, who liked to add a little bit of fruit to his mixes. This one had peach in it, which softened it to almost a vodka smoothness, and she thought of Antoinette's cousin Alexia, who proved herself to be a confidante and sometime crush-girl for Sunny, back in high school. Where Daddy's moonshine made her think of the harsh edges of Antoinette, the smooth, sweet notes of Jimmy's made her think about Alexia, and made her wonder what could have happened.

The heavy late evening air coated her skin and raised a layer of sweat, and it made her think about high school summers, and sleeping on the porch when it was too hot in the house, Gulf breezes offering a little relief. She took a sip, and savored it as it flowed down her throat.

A dark sedan pulled up in front of the house. Sunny stopped the swing's motion with her feet and watched as the driver's door opened and a woman emerged, wearing a tight black evening dress that accentuated her shoulders and chest. As she approached, the dress moved with her athletic frame in ways that took Sunny's imagination to places she probably shouldn't go.

"I'll be damned," Sunny said, loud enough for Alexia to hear. She set her drink on the floor and stood. "All dressed up and nowhere to go?"

Alexia laughed as she took the three steps onto the porch. "Give me a damn hug, Caldwell."

SUGAR AND 'SHINE

"Well, all right." She laughed as Alexia grabbed her and held her close for a few moments, and it felt way better than it should have.

"Mmm, girl." Alexia stood back and held Sunny at arm's length. "Military life has been good to you." She smiled. "And the real thing looks much better than a photo on Facebook."

"Well, clearly lawyering has been good to you. And your pictures do not do you justice at all." She was wearing her hair short these days. Shorter than Sunny had ever seen it, and it drew attention to her face, and her warm dark eyes and her inviting, full lips.

"Flattery will get you everywhere," Alexia said with a little purr. "Feel like some company? Or were you going to work until dawn, as Jimmy said he expected?"

Sunny laughed. "In his dreams. And I'd love your company. When did you get to town?"

"Last weekend. And you were supposed to let me know when you got in."

She gave her a sheepish shrug. "Guess I needed a couple of days to process." She motioned toward the house with her head.

"Oh, girl." She shook her head. "Sorry I got up in your business."

"Nah, it's okay. I was going to call you tomorrow."

Alexia's expression was pure skepticism and Sunny grinned.

"Really. I was. I always liked hanging out with you. That hasn't changed. Unless you're an asshole lawyer instead of a cool one and you've got me fooled."

"There are those who would say that I am the former."

"But I knew you when, so I can knock you right off that pedestal. Anyway, I'd offer you something to eat, but—"

"Oh, shit. I've got something. Hold on." She kicked her shoes off and jogged out to her car, leaving Sunny to wonder which was more incongruous. A woman who looked as elegant as Alexia cursing or running down the walk in an evening dress. It was kind of surprising, since she'd been so quiet in high school. But it was also kind of sexy.

Alexia returned, carrying a pie tin in one hand and her phone in the other.

"Oh, sweet Jesus. Is that your Aunt Mae's chess pie?" Sunny took the pie tin from her.

"She told me to bring what was left when I told her I was going to swing by. She said she'd make you another one, but you have to come by for a visit."

Sunny made a noncommittal noise. "You want to see the house?"

"I already have. Stopped by after I got in. Jimmy's doing an excellent job. Go get a couple of forks." She took a seat on the swing and put her phone on the floor. She gestured for Sunny to give her the pie tin back and Sunny handed it over.

"Be right back." Sunny went inside and pulled two plastic forks from their packet on the kitchen counter and took a Coke out of the fridge for Alexia. A few moments later she was seated next to her and she took the first bite.

"Oh, God, that's good." Chocolate. Alexia's aunt made it just right. Some chess pie was so sweet you could only eat a couple of bites before it overwhelmed you. But Aunt Mae's recipe ensured that you weren't sugar-highed until you had at least one whole piece. "Your aunt wins in chess pie, hands down."

Alexia laughed. "It is the best. My mama's is good, but Aunt Mae's always beats hers. They have throw-downs about it sometimes, but it's all in fun." She opened the bottle of Coke and took a swig then positioned the bottle between them. "So." She looked at her. "Jimmy said you're thinking about ditching the reunion."

Sunny didn't answer and instead took another bite, thinking that whatever cologne Alexia was wearing smelled good on her.

"You already said you'd go, Caldwell."

"Yeah, well, guess you don't remember high school all that well. I never really fit in."

"Oh, and I did," Alexia said with extra snark as she took a huge scoop of pie with her fork.

"A lot better than I did. You and Toni ran with the popular crowd. I'm from the wrong side of the tracks," she teased. "Cracker girl trying to hang out with the black debs."

"Like that's never happened here."

"Not much."

She gave her a look. "Please. Like my cousin even gave me the time of day unless it was convenient for her." Alexia looked at her. "She's not coming, by the way."

"Saw that on her Facebook page. Hope it's not 'cause I said I was."

"You know she'd show up if she could to see if she could talk you into bed again."

Sunny laughed. "You think?" She balanced a bite of pie on her fork. "It's been ten years."

Alexia took the pie tin back so she could take another bite. "I don't think. I know."

"Well, it wouldn't work this time."

"Oh? Why not?"

"Older, wiser, and I don't feel that way about her anymore."

Alexia coughed and it sounded like "bullshit."

"What?"

"Really? My incredibly gorgeous cousin wouldn't be able to talk you into bed again?"

"That was then, this is now. And you're just as gorgeous." More, actually, Sunny thought.

"Now. Maybe not then." Alexia scraped some of the pie off the side of the tin and Sunny remembered her in high school, a gawky, serious teen with braces who nevertheless could always make her laugh. She remembered one night halfway through their senior year at the Sonic with a group of friends. Alexia was telling a story about a date gone bad and she was laughing, but Sunny could tell it hurt, and she wanted to hug her, say it would be all right, and for some other reason she couldn't name at the time, she wanted to kiss her, too. She had that same feeling now, sitting there in the warmth of a summer night with the smell of magnolia and Alexia's cologne in the air.

"Here's the news she hasn't announced," Alexia said. "She's going through a divorce."

The fork stopped on the way to Sunny's lips. "Husband number two? Or did she sneak another one in there?"

Alexia smirked. "Two. It's a new development. It's not all over town yet."

"My lips are sealed."

Alexia laughed and took another drink. "She needs to get her shit together, as they say, and stop pretending she's straight."

"You mean like I did in high school?"

"You never pretended." Alexia held the tin so Sunny could take another bite. "You just kept your business to yourself."

"Maybe. Remember that time Aunt Mae almost caught us in the pool?"

"That was hilarious. After the fact."

"I owed you one for the diversion. And I had a huge bruise from jumping the fence." Sunny smiled about that summer day their senior year, when Antoinette talked her into skinny-dipping, among other things, in the pool at Alexia's house. Nobody was there at first, and they didn't hear when someone arrived. Alexia saw them first, signaled a warning, and kept her mom and aunt inside under some pretext while Sunny grabbed her clothes and hid behind the pool house where she dressed then climbed over the fence.

"Take that last bite," Alexia said, motioning at it with her fork.

"Are you sure?"

"Aunt Mae would kill me if she thought you didn't get enough."

"In that case…" Sunny scraped the last of the pie up and savored the last, glorious bite. "Mmm. So good."

"Bet a lot of girls have heard that."

Sunny was glad she had already swallowed because she was pretty sure she would've choked otherwise. She laughed as she set the tin with the forks on the porch, where it would be out of the way then grabbed the Mason jar while she was bent over and held it out. Alexia exchanged the Coke bottle for the Mason jar with a grin.

"I was just thinking about your daddy's moonshine." She took a sip. "But hot damn, this is not your daddy's. Did you make this?"

"No, it's one of Jimmy's batches." Sunny put the Coke bottle next to the pie tin.

"No disrespect to your daddy, but if this is what we had in high school, we probably would've gotten into a lot more trouble."

"Maybe we just appreciate the taste more now that we're older." She took the jar and sipped, wondering if she was putting her lips where Alexia's had been—she hoped so—and wanting the kind of trouble they could've gotten up to. "So how come you let me go on as long as I did with Toni?"

Alexia took the Mason jar from her. "You wouldn't have listened. Nobody did, when it came to her."

Sunny traced a seam between porch floor boards with her toe and watched the green flashes of fireflies over the front lawn in the darkness. "I felt kind of stupid for a while after senior year."

"You didn't need to. She probably told you things she thought she believed. Besides, we were young. Everybody's stupid at that age."

Sunny laughed, enjoying how Alexia's southern Alabama accent came on strong when she relaxed. She took the Mason jar back, her fingers bumping Alexia's. "Do you remember how fucked up we got after graduation?"

"Oh, my God. How the hell did I even get home?"

"I got you there. But I'm not sure how I got home after that. I hurt for three days."

"Same here." The Mason jar was almost empty, Sunny saw, in the last of the evening light. "Don't go anywhere." She went inside and filled it half-full again. "So I know you didn't get all dressed up for me," she said when she returned to the porch. "Did your mama have some kind of function?"

"This old thing?" Alexia teased. "I wore it just for you."

Sunny handed her the Mason jar. "Because you knew how good I look all tired out?"

Alexia chuckled. "You always look good, Caldwell. And yes. My mother and Aunt Mae had a fundraising dinner for a local candidate. And oh, my God, how I hate that shit. I hate dressing up and I hate having to pretend I'm happy to be there."

"You haven't changed all that much. You always hated that shit. But dressing up looks good on you."

She snorted. "I preferred hanging out with you and your friends." She took a swallow from the jar. "At least they didn't pretend to be something they weren't, or to enjoy something they didn't."

"Everybody pretends sometimes." Sunny took the jar and this time, she took a bigger swallow and liquid heat poured through her veins. Not quite a buzz, but on the way. And it mixed with another kind of heat that wrapped itself around her thighs, the kind that fed off Alexia's smile and her laugh and the liquid sound of her voice.

"Not like that."

"Money makes people weird."

Alexia laughed. "True. And I'm a hypocrite for dissing my people."

Sunny laughed, too, and handed her the jar. Alexia took a big swallow. "Careful, girl," Sunny teased. "Moonshine's a truth serum. You might tell me a deep, dark secret."

"I will tell you one. But first, I'm here to make sure you go to the reunion."

"I haven't decided."

"It's day after tomorrow. And you already signed up."

"And then I got here. Guess I got a little weird myself."

"So go with me. Two odds make an even."

Sunny grinned. "That's some crazy math," she hedged, but she liked the offer.

"One and one make two. An even."

She didn't respond.

"Caldwell." She handed Sunny the jar. "Go. With me."

Sunny sipped, and she thought about the times she and her friends would get together at the beach Saturday nights with cheap beer and Daddy's moonshine and hang out until just before the local cops did their rounds and then they'd head home, and she'd wonder why she was so different, and why all her crushes were on girls. The first person she'd told was Alexia, who had given her a big hug. She thought, and not for the first time, that maybe it should've been Alexia in the truck with her instead of Antoinette, that night during their junior year.

"Well?"

"What?" Sunny looked over at her, and she could just make out her features in the dark.

"Don't 'what' me. Go to the reunion with me. I'll even drive."

Sunny didn't respond. She took another sip, and she knew, in that moment, that she really needed to kiss Alexia Robinson.

"I'll tell you a deep, dark secret," Alexia said. "One that nobody knows."

Sunny laughed. "Bribery, now?"

"If that's what it takes."

"Okay. Better take another drink." She handed the jar to Alexia, who took a swallow.

"Here's my secret." She paused for effect. "I had a huge crush on you senior year."

Her words warmed Sunny's chest more than the moonshine. "I like that secret."

"But I didn't tell you, because you were all hung up on Toni."

"Not entirely, I wasn't."

"Oh, really?" Alexia smirked.

"Really."

"You made room for other women?" she teased.

Sunny shrugged noncommittally, enjoying the flirtatious digs.

"Who else?"

"If you're lucky, I'll show you."

"I'm feeling pretty lucky." She handed the moonshine back and Sunny laughed and moved a little closer on the swing, thinking now would be a really good time to kiss her, but then Alexia's phone rang.

"Shit. That's Mama."

"You're busy."

Alexia chuckled, low in her throat. "Not yet, but I'm hoping."

Sunny leaned in, a little closer, but the phone started ringing again.

Alexia sighed. "She won't stop. Let me deal with this." She retrieved her phone from the floor and stood, and suddenly the swing was a lot lonelier. Sunny leaned back, and though the night was warm, the heat she felt wasn't from that. Alexia brushed past her, talking on the phone, and she reached out and grazed Sunny's arm with her fingertips and they left goosebumps on her skin.

She watched Alexia move to the top of the porch stairs, and she remembered their graduation night, and how they'd gone to a few house parties and ended up dancing a little too close. She chalked it up to the alcohol though she knew it was way more than that, knew that something brewed between them, but neither of them acted on it, and neither even knew if they should. Glad that was then, Sunny thought. She knew damn well what she wanted to do now.

Alexia was trying to finish the conversation, from her body language, and finally she signed off and turned toward her. "That woman can talk more than a country preacher at an Easter service."

Sunny set the Mason jar on the floorboards and stood. "Did you tell her I said she still makes the best chess pie in the South?"

"Something like that. She wanted to know how you are."

"What did you say?" Sunny asked as she moved close enough to see the curve of Alexia's lips, even in the dark.

"That the last ten years look really good on you."

Sunny grinned. "They look amazing on you." She cupped Alexia's cheek with her hand and stroked her skin with her thumb and Alexia made a little sound and covered Sunny's hand with her own.

"I'm feeling pretty lucky, too," Sunny whispered and then she kissed her, and Alexia's lips were soft but insistent against hers, and she put her arms around Sunny's neck and pressed harder against her. Alexia's mouth tasted like moonshine and chocolate chess pie. Sunny ran her hands down her back, the silken fabric of her dress an invitation beneath her palms. Alexia had one hand wrapped around her and another in her hair and she kissed Sunny deeper, kissed her like she meant it, and like she wanted to do a whole lot of catching up.

"'Bout time, Caldwell," Alexia said against Sunny's mouth.

"Not like I was playing hard to get." She rested her hands on Alexia's hips and pulled her closer, enjoying the arousal that throbbed between her legs.

"The pie probably gave you a little more incentive."

Sunny laughed. "Nah. It's all you." All Alexia, with skin the color of that chocolate chess pie, who carried the last ten years like a damn trophy, and who made her want to do a hell of a lot more than just kiss.

"So what do you think?" Sunny asked.

"I think I want to know what I've been missing."

"I was hoping you'd say that." And Sunny led her inside and up the stairs, to the room that used to be hers, but that now smelled faintly of paint and floor sealant, even with one window open a little and the air conditioner droning from the other. Like a new house might, a house that didn't have any memories.

So Sunny unzipped Alexia's dress, let it fall, and ran her hands gently over her shoulders and down her arms. They'd make a memory, then. One that would make her smile on summer nights down the line, when she smelled magnolia and sea air or sipped moonshine and ate chess pie.

Alexia kissed her, and it was another round of dynamite in Sunny's chest, another wave of heat down her thighs, and she wondered why she'd gone so long without kissing Alexia Robinson or without letting her put her hands on her bare skin beneath her shirt. And then there were no clothes between them, and Sunny lowered Alexia to the bed, where she explored her from the hollow of her throat to the smooth muscles of her calves, then let Alexia do the same to her, let her add more heat and sweat to the night, let her slide her fingers inside and coax a rhythm from them both.

"Jesus," Sunny said with a gasp as Alexia thrust with her fingers and worked her clit with her thumb.

"Gettin' religious on me?" Alexia said near her ear.

"Gettin' something." Sunny kissed her hard, sucked her tongue into her mouth, and drew a moan from Alexia. And then there was only sensation, only Alexia's fingers and her mouth and her sweat-slicked skin as Sunny exploded, vaguely aware of Alexia collapsing against her.

"Damn," Alexia said with a soft laugh as she pulled out. "Maybe I should have said something senior year."

"Nah." Sunny gently sucked on her earlobe.

"Why not?"

"'Cause I'm much better at this now." She grinned and in a smooth motion she had Alexia under her.

"Really? Better show me."

"Yeah. I'd better." And she slowly but relentlessly touched Alexia in all the right places, spent long, delicious moments tasting her breasts and the salt and sweat between them, and worked her way lower until Alexia gasped and strained against her.

But Sunny teased her even more with her lips and then the tip of her tongue, savoring, until Alexia moaned and begged her to finish. Still Sunny teased, and when Alexia was so close Sunny could taste it, she slid her fingers in and kissed Alexia's mouth, hard and deep. Alexia wrapped her arms tight around her when she came, and she didn't let go as she shuddered and gasped and Sunny adjusted her position and waited a few moments for her to relax a little more. She did, and Sunny pulled out and Alexia snuggled against her.

"You're right," Alexia said after a while.

"About what?"

"Not saying anything senior year."

"Told you."

Alexia laughed. "And the night is still young."

"So I hope."

Then Alexia moved, and Sunny knew the night was indeed young, and by the time they lay, spent, in each other's arms, she was sure it was close to dawn. It had been a while, since she'd stayed up nearly all night with a woman. A long while. She kissed Alexia's shoulder, glad she was that woman.

"What time does Jimmy get here?" Alexia asked as she idly traced patterns on Sunny's back with her fingertip.

"Around ten. He has to go to Home Depot."

"I'm not planning to leave before that."

"Good." Sunny liked the way Alexia felt beneath her, liked the smell of sex and satiation between them.

"What are you going to tell him?"

"That you talked me into going to the reunion."

Alexia smiled and kissed her. "How long are you in town?"

"Another week, give or take. You?"

"About the same. And I think you need to stop by as soon as possible, get some more chess pie."

Sunny smiled and kissed her a few more times. "Look where that got me."

"Finally."

Sunny laughed.

"And bring some moonshine."

"You see the trouble that caused."

"Mmm. I'm looking to get in a lot more with you." She traced Sunny's lower lip with the tip of her tongue, and a delicious chill shot up Sunny's back. "And find out what else I missed the last ten years."

"Oh, you don't want to wait until the reunion to get all caught up?"

"Nice try, Caldwell. You're mine all week."

"That's a lot of chess pie," she said, with extra innocence.

"You really think I'll need it?" Alexia grasped Sunny's hips and moved against her, moved like there was a lot more to uncover.

"Nah," Sunny said with a grin and she knew for sure she'd be awake to see the sun rise. "It's all you."

Alexia cupped her face with one hand and stroked her lips with her thumb. And then she was kissing her again and Sunny lost herself, lost track of where her skin ended and Alexia's began, and by the time Alexia drowsed in her arms, as morning crept in through the partially open window, they'd made plenty of memories.

"Hey, Caldwell," Alexia mumbled against her neck.

"Yeah?"

"I'm really glad you're here."

She smiled. "Me, too." And she knew, in that moment, that she really needed to make a lot more memories with Alexia Robinson.

SUNNY'S SUMMER ROMANCE

Ingredients

1 southern Alabama night
1 porch swing
1 Mason jar of Jimmy's peach moonshine
half of Aunt Mae's chocolate chess pie
a little bit of a crush from back in the day
memories and fireflies

Directions

Start with the night. Add the swing. Sprinkle both with memories and fireflies. Stir in moonshine, slowly add bites of chess pie. Pour that crush in nice and easy, all over the other ingredients, so it heats up just right.

Mix it slow.
Serve it hot.
Take all night.

DESSERT

VANILLA EXTRACT

JOVE BELLE

ELANA ANSWERS THE DOOR WITH a spatula in her hand and barely gives Kelly a kiss before she says, "Leave your shoes by the door." Then she heads back into the apartment, leaving Kelly to find the way on her own.

Kelly doesn't know what she expected for their second date, but being abruptly dismissed at the front door isn't it. Of course, she learned enough from their first date, if she can even really call it that, to know better than to expect anything from Elana, let alone something that falls within the guidelines of convention.

Still, she slips off her shoes as she calls after Elana, "It's nice to see you, too."

And it is nice. Really nice, actually. She feels better than she has all week now that she's here, in Elana's apartment, and seeing her in a slightly less stressful setting than last time. She drops her jacket over the back of the sofa and follows the path Elana took.

Maybe she shouldn't be pursuing this situation. "Relationship" doesn't fit what it is, which is complicated at best and destined for heartache and disaster at worst. Still, she's helpless to do anything else because the pull of Elana is simply too much to ignore. If they crash and burn, so be it. She's determined to make it truly spectacular.

She finds Elana in the kitchen, holding a box of cake mix and glaring at the directions. She laughs, because, really, cake mix? "What are you doing?"

"What does it look like?" Elana stops glaring at the box long enough to glare at Kelly for a moment. "I'm baking you a cake."

Kelly takes the box from Elana and sets it as far out of reach as possible. The thought of Elana cooking for her is sweet, but cake from a box? No. Not going to happen. She wraps Elana in a full-body embrace and kisses her with every intention of making her forget about her baking plans. Elana kisses her back, sucking on her bottom lip, making Kelly sigh in a good way. Then Elana abruptly pulls away.

"Why are you trying to distract me?"

Kelly wipes the edge of her mouth with the side of her finger, a technique that both sharpens the edge of her lipstick and wipes away the saliva from their kiss. "Why are you trying to—" she almost says "poison me," but catches herself just in time. "Bake a cake?"

Elana looks to the side, focusing on a spot outside the window. "You know, I just thought...you made me cake, so..."

Kelly laughs and hugs Elana because could she be any cuter? "So you wanted to return the favor?"

"Yeah."

Technically, Kelly hadn't made a cake for Elana. She'd made a wedding cake for Elana's brother. Elana had crashed the wedding because David, her brother, was marrying Elana's ex-girlfriend, Brittney. The promise of champagne and wedding cake that didn't "taste like ass"—Elana's words, not Kelly's—

was the only reason Elana had attended the reception as well. At least that's what Kelly chose to believe. The inconvenient reality that Elana is maybe—definitely—still hung up on Brittney is not something she wants to think about.

"Okay, and you thought a mix was the way to go?"

Elana grumbles something under her breath that sounds distinctly like "bastard cake conspiracy," but Kelly can't be sure, so she just shakes it off and prods Elana until she smiles. "Whatever, it seemed like a good idea."

"Of course it did." Then, because Elana still looks sad, she says, "It still is. Can I help?"

Elana waves her hand in a helpless, bordering-on-pathetic gesture and says, "I wanted to do it for you."

"Well, I could just…" Kelly checks the temperature on the oven and lowers it from 450 to 350. "Supervise."

"What do you mean?" Elana looks at her suspiciously.

"First lesson of cake making." Kelly picks up the box of mix and shakes it. "Nothing good ever came out of one of these." She tosses it in the trash and is tempted to go through Elana's cupboards to see if there are any others, but decides that might be rude.

"Hey! I paid good money for that!"

Kelly raises an eyebrow, but she doesn't move so that Elana can retrieve the mix from the trash. She's seen those mixes in the store. They cost around a buck. "Good money?"

Elana glares at her, but doesn't answer. Kelly kisses her because she really is too cute, especially when she's trying to be all severe. "Stop glaring. You don't get to be mad when I'm saving you from cake that tastes like ass."

Elana laughs and finally kisses her like she really means it. When the kiss ends, she rests her forehead against Kelly's and says, "I really missed you this week."

The admission makes Kelly's stomach dance and flop and then fall all the way to the floor. She likes the feeling, along with the sure, needy press of Elana's body against hers.

"Yeah?"

Elana nods, her forehead rolling against Kelly's in a way that makes her want to laugh, but she doesn't because the moment is far too serious for that. She wants Elana to trust her, trust that she won't make her regret showing her vulnerability.

"Is it too soon for me to admit that?" Elana's body tenses while she waits for Kelly's answer. Kelly rubs her hands over Elana's back, trying to smooth out her worries while she considers her answer.

Finally, she simply says, "I don't know, but I missed you, too."

The tension eases out of Elana's body and Kelly congratulates herself for getting the right answer on the first try.

"So, about that cake..." Elana smiles, and the room feels somehow lighter than it did the moment before.

"Let's just see what you have."

Kelly looks through Elana's cupboards and tries to keep a straight face, but it's almost impossible. She does okay at not reacting to the bleached white flour, which totally makes her shiver on the inside, but when she finds the imitation vanilla, she can't hold back any longer.

She tosses the flavoring into the trash, too, and looks at Elana with an expression that she hopes conveys disgust, disbelief, and a dash of "I dare you to complain about this." She has some hard lines when it comes to her relationships. She just can't be intimate with someone who has imitation vanilla in her house, let alone someone who would defend it.

Elana looks irritated, but she doesn't complain. That's good, because Kelly really likes her. She'd hate to end their—whatever this is—before it even gets started.

Kelly turns off the oven. "We need to go to the store."

"Seriously? You just threw my shit away and now I have to buy more?"

"Elana, you can't possibly expect me to make a cake using these ingredients."

"No, I expect you to let me make the cake."

"Fine, but we still need the right ingredients."

Elana sighs and Kelly holds her breath. Elana's either about to kick her out or grab her keys so they can go shopping.

"Is this what it's going to be like?" Elana asks.

"What?"

"To date a caterer. Or are you this big a pain in the ass over everything?"

"You'll thank me the next time you host a party and don't give your guests food poisoning," Kelly answers dryly.

"Are you going to be around long enough to cook for them?" And that touch of vulnerability is back in her eyes and all the potential fight leaves Kelly.

"I would like to be."

Elana nods decisively and grabs her keys. "Come on, then. This cake won't make itself."

They have to buy every single ingredient because Elana really has no idea what the difference between organic and GMO is. Kelly shakes her head, pays for the groceries because it's a hell of a lot more than the ninety-nine cents Elana spent on the cake mix. On sale.

"From now on," Kelly says, "we're eating at my house."

It would have been easier, she supposes, to have just taken Elana there today, where she already has all the proper ingredients to bake a cake, but her kitchen is special. It's *her* place. When life gets wonky, as it sometimes does, everything seems to correct itself when she's there. As much as she really likes Elana, and really wants to see where things will go between them, it's just too soon to take her there. She doesn't even know why she made the comment about eating at her place in the future. It was out of character and part of her hopes that Elana missed it completely. Another part of her hopes Elana heard it and likes the idea. It's more than she wants to contemplate, so she kisses Elana to distract them both. It works.

When they get back to Elana's place, after a completely inappropriate, yet really fun, make-out session in the New Season's parking lot, Elana lines the items they bought up on her counter. She looks at them skeptically.

"How is this better than—" she reaches in the pantry and pulls out another cake mix, "this?"

Kelly takes the mix—she *knew* there were others—and throws it in the trash on top of the other one. "How many of those do you have?"

Elana glares and crosses her arms. "I'm not telling."

Kelly smiles and pulls Elana close. "I promise, you won't need another cake mix as long as I'm around."

Elana bites her bottom lip and looks like she wants to say something, but finally she just nods. Kelly nudges her with her hip and says, "Okay?"

Elana shrugs and gives a small smile. "Okay."

"Good. Now, do you want to bake a cake?"

Elana looks at the ingredients suspiciously, but she nods anyway. "Show me what to do."

Kelly guides Elana through setting the oven, then starts up a narrative about the ingredients, about how they're different and better than the cheaper alternatives. Elana doesn't look convinced when Kelly explains the difference between organic baking flour and bleached, all-purpose flour and Kelly can't blame her. They don't look that different. Kelly knows the difference, trusts her years of experience, but it's apparently all new information for Elana.

When it's time to mix everything into a batter, Elana looks bored and a little annoyed, so Kelly takes over. Instead of the hand mixer that Elana produces, she opts to mix it by hand with a wooden spoon. It takes longer, of course, but she's a purist about some things.

"I still don't see what the big deal is." Elana sips from the glass of wine she'd poured when they'd started. Until this point, it's gone untouched because she's been too busy following instructions to drink. Kelly, on the other hand, has gone through two glasses and is ready for her third. She stirs the batter with exaggerated motions, lifting the spoon high and letting the batter run like a waterfall back into the bowl.

"It's not a big deal," Kelly agrees, "if you don't care how your cake tastes when it comes out of the oven."

"I can't even tell the difference between these ingredients." Elana says with a sniff.

"No? How about this?" Kelly opens the vanilla extract. Maybe the flour is hard to distinguish, but even someone whose staple diet comes out of a microwave can tell the difference between imitation and actual vanilla extract. She waves the bottle under Elana's nose. "Smell."

Elana inhales and her eyes roll back a little. "Wow. *That's* vanilla, huh?"

Kelly nods, then dips a finger in the batter. "Taste this."

Elana draws her finger into her mouth, licking and sucking and every other unholy thing she can do with her mouth until Kelly's eyes are rolling back into her head and she's moaning about how good it feels.

It's not just the texture of Elana's tongue against her finger, which is totally erotic, but it's more the look on her face, the way her eyes darken and she grasps Kelly's hand to hold it in place as she works her tongue until there's nothing left but her saliva on Kelly's fingers and an almost unbearable throbbing between Kelly's legs.

Kelly pulls her finger away reluctantly. "You like?"

"Mmm, I like." Elana insinuates herself into Kelly's space, so close that Kelly wonders if they've somehow managed to meld together, clothes and all, but she doesn't have time to think about it because Elana kisses her and all she can do is grab onto the edge of the counter behind her and hold on tight.

It's different than their previous kisses, more complete, more inspired, more like a mixing of emotions, than an attempt to cover them. She's not sure what caused it, exactly, since nothing really has changed. David is still Elana's brother, and she is still sorting through her very, very messy feelings for Brittney, David's new wife. Still, as Elana clutches Kelly's collar in one hand and cups her cheek in the other, her tongue barely glancing over her lips, Kelly feels like all that doesn't matter. Not in this moment, not with Elana whimpering in a way that completely dismantles her as she sucks on Elana's bottom lip.

She doesn't think about the cake batter on the counter or that the oven beeped a few minutes ago to alert that it's up to temperature or that she really should get the cake in to bake.

All she can think about is the way Elana *feels* and how much more she wants to feel if only she can convince her fingers to release the countertop and take hold of her. It's harder than it seems, because she's gripping the granite like it holds all of life's important secrets and she's afraid she'll hurt Elana if she holds onto her like that.

Elana fumbles with the button on Kelly's jeans, her hands brushing against the over-sensitized skin of her stomach, making her jump. When Elana gives up and pushes her hand into her pants without unfastening them, Kelly finally gives up her hold on the counter to help Elana. She's shaking and can't quite catch her breath, but she really, *really* wants her pants off. She loosens the button just as Elana's fingers brush over her clit, scrambling and searching lower until she's sliding inside of Kelly.

"God—" Kelly forgets about her pants and closes her eyes, unable to do anything except throw her head back and plead for more. "Yes, please."

Her voice is breathy and her words are a mess, but she knows Elana hears her by the way her mouth curves into a smile against her skin. Elana laughs, then sucks hard right where her neck curves into her shoulder as she strokes into Kelly. The penetration is abortive and not very effective because Elana's movement is so restricted by her pants, but it still draws a moan from somewhere deep inside Kelly.

Elana withdraws her hand with a frustrated growl. "I need to get these off." She pushes against the jeans, forcing the zipper open and they inch down her hips. "Help me." She punctuates the demand with her teeth against Kelly's clavicle.

Kelly pushes her pants and panties as far down her legs as she can. If she doesn't get Elana back inside her *right now*, she's going to cry with frustration. Only having her pants around her knees is actually worse because now she can't spread her legs and she's absolutely certain that clothes are the universe's way of punishing her for a crime she's completely forgotten about. She should have worn a skirt.

Elana pushes them down the rest of the way and Kelly steps out of one leg, but doesn't have time to step out of the other before Elana is inside her again. She clutches Elana's shoulders, her fingers digging in a little too hard because she's afraid she'll fly apart completely if she doesn't hold on.

"You feel so *good*," Elana groans as she scissors her fingers inside Kelly, fluttering them against the front wall until Kelly is writhing against her hand and begging her to do more.

She's not sure how they got here. One minute, she's stirring cake batter and Elana is watching with a dark look on her face. The next, her pants are crumpled around her ankles and Elana is fucking her so hard that all she can think about is coming. It's been a week since they met and fucked for the first time. Since then, she hasn't been able to forget how good it felt, how good it *feels,* to have Elana consume her like she is the only thing in the world.

"Yes." It's the only word Kelly knows, the only one she can think and send reliably from her brain to her mouth, so she says it over and over again as the pressure builds inside her. She can feel the orgasm, gathering and growing, ready to be released, but she grits her teeth and holds it back because she wants the feeling to last as long as possible.

"Stop fighting me." Elana sucks hard on her neck and it's going to take some serious makeup to cover the mark tomorrow, but Kelly doesn't care.

She doesn't know if it's the words, or the fingers thrusting inside of her, or Elana's mouth on her skin, but it's all too much. Before she's ready, before she can even draw a breath, she's pulled under by the tide, her lungs tight and ready to burst. She explodes at the bottom of the dive and floats back to the surface, her body fracturing into pieces until little by little, she feels herself coming back together. She can barely catch her breath as her body tries to reconstruct itself.

"You're so fucking sexy when you come." Elana's words reach her through the fog in her brain and she smiles and kisses Elana in response because there's no way she can actually talk right now.

She gives herself a moment to recover, to let herself coalesce, then she pushes away from the counter and drops to her knees. She doesn't have the energy or the wherewithal to fuck Elana like she just fucked her, but that doesn't eliminate all her options.

"What are you doing?" Elana laughs and plays with her hair, but her hips hitch just a little when Kelly grips her waist.

"I just need a second to recover. In the meantime, take these off." She tugs on a belt loop, hyperaware that her own pants are still connected to her by one leg. If she had more energy, she'd care about that, except for the part where all she really cares about right now is getting Elana naked. From the waist down, at least. She's starting to want that quite a lot.

Elana laughs again, but she loosens the button on her jeans and lowers the zipper. She draws it out, opening the teeth of the zipper so slowly, Kelly can hear them clicking one by one and she's just about got enough energy to do something drastic to correct it. For the moment, she's willing to let Elana tease her. She's still panting and trying to get the edges of her thoughts to clear, so the pace lets her build up her energy.

"Sure you're up for this?" Elana's tone is teasing, but the look in her eyes says she damn well better be. Kelly gets a brief, startling image of Elana stroking herself to orgasm while she watches. As much as she would enjoy that—a lot—her pride dictates that she hold herself a little higher. Apparently, she looks as wrecked as she feels, but she's insulted by the implication that she can't take care of Elana's needs.

"I'll show you *up for this.*" She pushes herself forward and jerks Elana's pants down. Her movements aren't smooth at all and she pulls so hard, she almost knocks Elana off balance. Somehow, flattening Elana through her clumsiness doesn't deter either of them. Elana struggles harder to get her clothes off and Kelly just gives up completely. Elana is exposed enough that Kelly can smell how turned on she is and that means she has to taste her. Now.

She can barely reach Elana's clit with her tongue, but it's enough to make Elana shudder and grab the counter the way Kelly had to. Suddenly, she's the one laughing and Elana's the one whimpering for more and it just feels so good to be with her. She knows they're going to have to deal with the bigger issues involving her brother and Brittney, but it seems less impossible than it did a week ago.

She looks up at Elana and meets her gaze. "I'm really glad I met you."

Elana huffs, but she smiles softly and it's a weird combination, but Kelly thinks she understands why. Anything else would too clearly show her as vulnerable and even though that's all Elana was the last time they were together, this time she wants to be stronger. Not that she's said any of that, so Kelly could be way off, but it's a nice thought.

"I'd be happier I met you if you'd get your mouth on me." Elana wiggles her hips and her pants drop a little farther.

Kelly wants to do this right, without the frustration of too many clothes in her way, so she summons her energy, which isn't actually too hard after watching Elana move while panting out her desires, and helps Elana properly remove her pants and panties. She's dying to "get her mouth on her," as Elana put it, but she also really wants to do it the right way.

As soon as the last scrap of underwear clears Elana's body, Kelly hitches Elana's leg over her shoulder and allows herself to simply indulge. She's a chef, a successful one at that, and maybe that makes her more sensitive to aromas and textures and flavors and how they all work together to make a perfect experience, but whatever the reason, she knows with the first brush of her tongue that this couldn't possibly get any better.

Elana groans and it's this deep, throaty, wild noise that makes Kelly pin her hips to the counter and thrust her tongue inside of her. She knows that being tongue fucked isn't as sexy as it sounds, but it's so amazingly dirty and intimate and there is no other way to match how Elana makes her feel when she grabs her hair and thrusts into her face.

"God...just...yes..." Elana talks her through it, encouraging her to move left or right or faster or harder, and all the words merge into one long moan that says Kelly is touching her in all the right ways.

She pulls away for a moment because her only options are to suffocate—which she considers doing until the burn in her lungs says she has to breathe right now—or stop briefly so she won't pass out before Elana finishes.

Elana groans in disappointment, her whole body coiled so tight that Kelly's not quite sure how to touch her because she might snap at any moment. Not that it stops her. She still holds Elana tight by the hips, her fingers leaving impressions in her skin, as she sucks in air and promises that she's not stopping.

She licks this time, because really, there's just no way her tongue is long enough or hard enough to make Elana come, no matter how amazing it feels. Not to mention, Elana's clit is right there and it's so freaking hard and poking out and Kelly has no choice but to flatten her tongue and hum her approval against it.

Elana jerks and swears in Spanish, and Kelly keeps on licking until Elana collapses on top of her, panting and begging her to stop and keep going all at once.

When they've both recovered sufficiently to speak, but not so completely that Kelly isn't still thrumming with arousal, Elana laughs and says, "No wonder my cakes don't taste as good as yours."

Kelly is a little bit insulted because Elana should not be able to form complete sentences like that. Not yet. And she certainly shouldn't be up for teasing, but she also knows that Elana just came like crazy because she's still wearing the evidence of the orgasm on her lips and chin.

As much as she wants to immediately go another round and take care of Elana's pesky ability to still think clearly, she's also acutely aware that the oven is still on and the cake batter is still sitting on the counter. She can't just leave it there forever. So she settles for smacking Elana on the ass, and then dragging herself to her feet with a sigh.

As she washes her hands and her face, she wonders if Elana isn't going to teach her more about baking a cake than the other way around. Ultimately she decides, as she pours the batter into the pan and then slides it into the oven, that it doesn't really matter who teaches what. The important part is that this isn't the last cake they will bake together.

VANILLA CAKE

Ingredients

2 1/2 cups unbleached all-purpose flour

2 1/4 teaspoons baking powder

1/4 teaspoon salt

1 cup whole milk

1 teaspoon vanilla extract

2 cups granulated sugar

4 eggs

Frosting of your choice

Directions

1. Preheat oven to 350° F. Grease bottom and sides of two 9-inch round cake pans, line bottoms with parchment paper, then grease the paper.

2. Sift together flour, baking powder, and salt. In a medium bowl, mix together milk and vanilla.

3. In a large mixing bowl, beat sugar and eggs together with a wooden spoon until blended and slightly thickened. Alternate adding flour and milk mixtures, blending in each addition. Beat just until batter is smooth (work out any lumps)—don't overbeat. Pour into the prepared pans.

4. Bake for 30 to 40 minutes or until tops are golden and a toothpick inserted in center comes out clean. Rotate pans halfway through. Transfer to cooling racks and let cool for 5 minutes. Invert cakes onto racks and remove parchment. Let cool completely. Frost with your favorite frosting.

Makes two 9-inch cakes.

SMORGASBORD

R.G. EMANUELLE

Renee surveyed the smorgasbord on her dining room table. Truffles, spreads and pestos of various colors, and buttery vegetables were laid out within reach.

She stuck a finger in the hummus and scooped some out. With the very tip of her tongue, she tasted it, then flung it onto the canvas, also lying on the table. She regarded the splatters for a moment, then scooped up a handful of steamed baby peas and dropped them, one by one, over the hummus.

She stepped back and stared at the canvas. No, this wasn't right. She rubbed her forehead, hoping to dispel both the headache and frustration of the past two weeks, filled with fits and starts on this project.

Renee sighed and decided that she needed a break. She'd go to the art show she'd been invited to. Quickly, she threw on something clean and presentable and left her project in the dark.

Renee walked around the gallery, briefly studying each piece displayed on the walls. She was only mildly interested in this particular artist, but the show got her out for a while. She was more captivated by the bold Malbec in her hand and the Manchego at the cocktail station.

After an hour, she began looking for a way to escape unobtrusively. But there was only one exit, and the artist was squarely in front of it.

A thick blanket of pretentiousness in the room was smothering her and she decided to step outside for air. The gallery's garden was flanked on two sides by large oak trees, and stone benches dotted the perimeter. Chinese lanterns illuminated the area with a soft light.

The garden was usually a popular place for people who needed air or a smoke, but tonight there were only three others, and when Renee walked out, two of them went back inside the gallery.

A lone woman sat on a bench, sipping a glass of red and staring at a vine of climbing roses. Her hair was set in two braids of black with streaks of blood red through them, echoing the wine in her hand. The movement of her breathing made her glass sparkle with refracted light.

What to say to such a beautiful woman? Maybe she was hungry. A good woman never refused food.

Renee dashed back inside and moved quickly through the crowds of art-lovers until she spotted a server holding up a tray. The server, evidently seeing her look inquisitively, smiled and lowered the tray. "Mushroom en croute?"

"Yes, please." Renee took a napkin off the tray and picked up two of the little dumplings, placed them on the napkin, and returned to the garden. Back outside, she took a deep breath and walked over to the woman. She was now looking at a stone fountain sculpted into a woman in flowing robes emptying a bucket into a pool.

Renee approached her cautiously, not wanting to startle her, but she did anyway. The woman jumped a little as she turned. "Oh!"

"I'm sorry," Renee said, feeling a bit startled herself. "You looked like you could use a little something." She held out her hand with the mushroom en croute, slightly smashed. She hadn't realized that she'd squeezed them. "Oh," she said, embarrassed. "I'm really sorry. These were good-looking a minute ago."

The woman chuckled. "It still looks good, just a little more…rustic."

Renee's heart skipped a beat. It wasn't often she met a woman at these functions who had a genuine sense of humor.

"Thank you." The woman took one of the hors d'oeuvre and shoved the entire thing in her mouth, then daintily whisked away the flaky crumbs around her lips. Not what Renee was expecting, but cute.

"Well, how is it?" she asked.

"Not bad. Try it."

Renee popped the other one into her mouth. "Mmm."

"I'm Delilah." She put her hand out.

Delilah? How poetic.

"Renee." She took Delilah's hand and had a vision of pulling her up and out of there, taking her where they could be alone, away from these people.

"Do you want to sit?" Delilah scooted over.

Renee sat, suddenly aware that she had lost her Malbec and had probably put it down when she'd gone back inside.

She motioned a server who was going around with bellinis. When she'd gotten one, she asked, "So, what do you do?"

"I'm a writer."

"Are you covering the installation?"

"No, I'm here because my co-worker scored me an invitation. I have a food column in *The Tribune.*"

Renee turned her whole body toward Delilah. "*The Tribune?* You're Delilah Ramsey? I read your column all the tim" She put her drink down on the bench.

Delilah blushed. "Thanks." She scanned Renee's hands and arms, crossed loosely against her chest, and stopped at her face. Renee could feel each part turning red, as if Delilah were searing her skin with her gaze.

Renee gripped the carved stone beneath her to keep from sliding off. Delilah's green eyes were deep and multilayered, with hints of wisdom, like she'd lived twenty lives.

"Are you a foodie?" Delilah asked.

"I suppose." Renee chuckled. "I work with food."

"Really? Are you a chef?"

"No."

"Then how so?"

"I use food as part of my art."

Delilah's eyes narrowed a bit and her voice lowered when she said, "I'd love to see some of your work."

Renee swallowed. "Um, sure. I'd love to show you."

Delilah regarded her a moment and Renee felt herself flare with heat. "You looked as bored as I was when you walked out here. How's about we go now?"

"Now?" Renee suddenly felt ill.

Delilah peered around Renee to look through the glass doors and into the gallery. Inside, artists were chatting with patrons and reporters, flutes of Champagne in their hands, everyone dressed in customary black. "Yes. Let's blow this popsicle stand."

Renee's apartment was sparsely furnished, the space taken up by canvases, sculptures, and artists' paraphernalia.

"Wow, look at all this light," Delilah said.

"Yeah, that's what I love about this place. The natural light is great. But, as you can see, the place isn't that big. I'm going to move soon."

"I know what you mean. I need an entire room for all my cooking equipment."

Renee slung her jacket over a chair. "Would you like some coffee? Or a drink?"

"Coffee would be great."

She went into the kitchen, which was separated from the rest of the apartment only by a bar-style counter.

While the coffee dripped, Delilah walked around the loft, pausing at different pieces of art to study them. Many of them used food as either a subject or medium. She stopped at a framed painting of a beachscape in which orange slices splayed across the horizon. "This is fantastic. You're very creative."

"Well, so are you. Those recipes you come up with always sound so delicious."

"Yes, but you take food to a whole new level. I never would've thought to use orange slices like this." She admired it for another moment. "How do you keep the food from rotting? Do you spray something on it?"

"Yes. It's a special varnish. A couple of coats, and food is preserved indefinitely."

"Like a bug in amber."

Renee laughed. "Yeah, I suppose."

She poured two mugs of coffee and placed them on the counter. "I've only got half-and-half. Hope that's okay."

"Absolutely. I don't understand skim milk in coffee." Delilah walked over to the counter and sat on one of the stools. She frowned. "Makes it look and taste like dirty bath water. Delish."

Renee's chest fluttered. A foodie, a sense of humor, and sarcasm. *Now, if only she's into music, she'd be my dream woman.* "Do you like music?"

"Love it. What do you like?"

"A little of everything. Rock, dance, jazz, blues, alternative."

"Me, too! My favorite, though, is slow and soulful. Like Joss Stone."

She's Venus. I've just met Venus. "I think I have some cookies somewhere."

"No, thanks. You're sweet enough."

Renee's ears rang as blood rushed to her head. Was she still in an upright position?

"So, tell me about what's going on over there." Delilah pointed her chin in the direction of the table with the canvas lying on it.

"I'm working on a project. After the positive reactions I got on my last installation, *Culinary Adventures* magazine wants me to do a photo project. But it's not working. I keep trying different things, but it's just not happening."

"Why are you having such a hard time?"

"I don't know. Something's missing."

"Well, what exactly are you doing?"

"I'm preparing certain foods and using them as the paint on the canvas."

"How avant-garde of you." She looked over at the table. "What kinds of foods?"

"For this one, chocolate—both in truffle and ganache form—a fava bean spread, hummus, cherries, cilantro pesto..." Renee started to feel foolish. Delilah must think she's nuts.

"That sounds sexy."

"That's good. I was going for sexy."

"Well, I'm not that experienced with art, but I'd be happy to brainstorm with you...if that would help."

Renee wasn't sure how to respond. On the one hand: beautiful woman, willing to spend time with her and discuss her work. On the other hand: total stranger.

"I'd love that. Maybe we can have dinner sometime?" Renee tried to look casual by sipping her coffee.

"How about this Friday?"

Renee's throat went dry. She took another swig. Hot coffee, she discovered, does nothing to help moisten a parched throat. "I—yes, I'd love to."

"Great." Delilah smiled, then looked at her watch. "I'm afraid I have to go. I have a dinner date at nine." She slid off the stool and picked up her cup.

Renee gestured for her to leave it. "Okay." She tried not to sound disappointed. "Um, I should give you my number."

"No need. I'll pick you up Friday at seven, okay?"

Good God, this woman was sweeping her off her feet. She tried to control her smile so that it didn't turn into a dumb-ass grin. "Sounds intriguing. I'm looking forward to it."

"Me, too." She pulled her jacket on and picked up her purse. "Thanks for the coffee."

"Anytime," Renee replied, as Delilah walked out her door.

Renee had never been the type to go through her entire wardrobe looking for the right outfit for a date, but tonight she must have pulled out every shirt, skirt, and pair of pants and tried them on with every pair of shoes. She had to hurry, though—she had just buzzed Delilah up.

It occurred to her at some point that she had no idea where Delilah was taking her. A fancy place? Casual? Pizza? She finally decided on something neutral—a pair of gray slacks and a royal blue button-down blouse. She was fastening a simple chain-link silver necklace when the doorbell rang. Her hands began trembling and she lost her grip on the clasp. She tried a couple more times but couldn't keep it open. The doorbell rang again.

"Damn!" She ran out with the chain in her hand and stopped at the door for a second to regain her composure, then opened it.

Delilah stood there wearing black jeans and motorcycle boots and a black pull-over with a collared white shirt. Okay, casual.

"Hi," Renee said.

"Hi. You ready?"

"Sure. Let me just grab my jacket. Come in for a sec."

While Delilah waited by the door, Renee attempted once more to get the chain around her neck. She struggled for a minute before Delilah came over. "Here, let me help you." She took the chain and brought it around Renee's throat. Renee felt her fingers on the nape of her neck and she shivered, hoping that it wasn't obvious. When Delilah had clasped the chain, her fingers remained on Renee's skin—only for a second or two, but enough to make Renee's belly tighten.

"Thanks." Renee put her jacket on. "Okay, let's go."

Despite her angst, the car ride was surprisingly comfortable. Their conversation was so natural that Renee didn't pay attention to where they were going, and before long, Delilah pulled up at a curb.

"Here we are."

Renee looked out the window. They had parked in front of a row of brick houses. She didn't see a restaurant. "Here?"

"Yeah." Delilah got out of the car and went up on the sidewalk, where she waited for her. Renee followed.

"Um, where's the restaurant?"

"This way." Delilah led her up the block a couple of yards and turned in toward a pinkish brick house with an iron fence enclosing a little shrub garden. She led Renee up the driveway to a side door, and up a flight of stairs.

Delilah kept silent until they reached the top and walked into a vestibule. From there, they entered a dining room.

A rectangular, rough-hewn wooden table was prepared with two place settings, wine glasses, and candles. A round, squat vase filled with white chrysanthemums sat in the center.

"Oh, wow," Renee said. "What is this?"

"This is the restaurant. It's called Delilah's Kitchen," she said with a playful grin.

Renee was stunned. Women had cooked dinner for her, but never as a surprise like this. "I don't know what to say."

"Well, don't just stand in the doorway. Come in."

Renee walked cautiously toward the table, afraid to disturb anything.

On the table was a platter of what looked like artichoke hearts and a bottle of Chenin blanc. "I feel terrible. I didn't bring anything. Why didn't you tell me? I would've brought wine or dessert or—"

"Everything tonight is on me, including the wine and dessert."

Renee stood motionless. A strange sensation rippled through her, like a combination of settling into a warm blanket on a cold wintry day and sticking your finger in a light socket. She went to the entrance of the kitchen. Equipment filled almost every inch of space. "That is the biggest food processor I've ever seen in my life," she said.

"I bet you say that to all the girls."

"Actually, I don't," Renee responded with a snort.

Delilah nodded. "Yeah, I kind of have a weakness for kitchen toys. And anyway, I do so much cooking, it pays to have the good stuff." She shrugged. "Why don't you open up the wine? I'll finish up in here. We'll eat soon."

Renee went back to the table, picked up the corkscrew, and began working on the bottle. "Well, not too soon, I hope." Her voice caught slightly.

Delilah joined her and bent over to pick up the two wine glasses. She moved closer to her, holding them up. "Do you have somewhere to be after dinner?"

"No."

"Then we've got all night."

Renee's hand trembled slightly as she poured the wine.

"Let's go sit in the living room while the food finishes cooking."

They sat on her couch, an intimate thing that would have held three people at most. "Here's to new friends," Delilah said, holding up her glass.

"To new friends." Renee clinked her glass against Delilah's and sipped. She needed the fortification.

Delilah brought her knees up and rested her feet on the couch. Her living room was simple, with a couple of pieces of artwork on the walls and a few decorative items here and there.

Over the wine, they chatted about Renee's work and her methods until a rich, savory aroma began to waft in.

"Oh, my god, something smells amazing. What is that?"

"Swedish meatballs."

Renee looked at her sideways. "You are a goddess."

Delilah laughed. "Hardly. It's not as complicated as people think. At least, my version isn't."

In the moment of silence that followed, and under Delilah's gaze, Renee felt as if nothing else in the world existed. There was only here and now.

The spell was broken when Delilah got up. "I think they're ready."

Renee followed her out. "Can I help?"

"Absolutely not. Have a seat at the table."

"I feel funny not doing anything. I mean, you cooked dinner—"

"I've got it under control."

Renee sat down at the table. Two bamboo placemats held white square plates and cloth napkins folded into wooden napkin rings. "You set a beautiful table," she called out to the kitchen.

"Thank you," Delilah responded, as she brought in a small platter. She set it on the table and sat down. "Please, help yourself."

Renee picked up two of the little meatballs by the toothpicks sticking out of them and put them on her plate. Delilah then picked up the artichokes. "Try these."

"They look great." She took a spoonful of the hearts. She tasted raspberry vinaigrette.

Dinner conversation was light and comfortable as they made their way through Delilah's menu: Trofie with pesto, blackened catfish with red quinoa, and sauteed bok choy.

"You know," Delilah said after they'd eaten everything on their plates, "I'd like to do a story on you. An artist who uses food in her art. Not just in the usual way, like crushing berries for paint, but actually using food in the art."

"Um, okay."

"I hope you left room for dessert. I made it fresh."

"You *made* dessert, too?"

"Of course." She batted her eyes coquettishly. "Why don't you go into the living room? I'll bring dessert in there."

Within a couple of minutes of settling on the couch, Delilah entered with two sundae glasses in her hands. "Chocolate Kahlua pudding."

Renee's jaw dropped. "Oh. My. God. You can't be serious."

Delilah placed them on the coffee table. "You seem to have a predilection for chocolate."

They both scooped spoonfuls into their mouths. Renee closed her eyes and moaned. "This is incredible," she murmured.

Delilah smiled. "It's one of my signature dishes. I've made it a thousand times. Funny, I was worried it wouldn't come out right."

"Why?"

Delilah blushed and Renee melted.

"I really wanted it to come out good for you."

The pudding was soft and warm and it made her think of Delilah's flesh, shoulders, breasts, and possibly touching all of them with her lips. She quickly stuck another spoonful in her mouth.

"I love chocolate, too," Delilah continued. "There's something so sensual about it. It's smooth, silky, rich, and complex. And, of course, chocolate triggers endorphins. It's a known aphrodisiac."

Renee swallowed. "Does that mean you're trying to seduce me?"

The air in the room became laden with suggestion. They stared at each other for a long moment. Renee looked at her braids, following the path of one red streak, weaving in and out of the ropes of hair, winding like a river. Then both began nervously laughing. Delilah dribbled pudding onto her shirt and she wiped it, still laughing.

"Uh-oh, I hope that comes out."

"It's okay, I'm used to spilling food on myself."

Renee watched her calmly dab her shirt with her napkin, and it dawned on her. The thing her project was missing.

"Would you be willing to help me with my project?"

Delilah's eyes widened. "I'd love to! What do you need me to do?"

Renee told her what she had in mind. Although Delilah seemed hesitant at first, she agreed.

Despite the incredible dinner she'd just had, Renee felt ill again. Thinking about what she was going to do with Delilah was almost too much to think about.

Three days later, Delilah sat at Renee's counter in a robe with her laptop and began her story while Renee prepared her workspace.

Renee draped a drop cloth over the dining room table and smoothed it out. "Okay, lie down." Delilah untied the robe and slowly let it drop off her shoulders and slide down her body. Renee swallowed hard. Delilah was stunning, from the curve of her plump breasts to her smooth thighs. For a second, she wondered what it would be like to lay her head down on those breasts after a long, hard day. Her full thighs and curvaceous hips would make a sumptuous canvas.

As Delilah lay down, her hair settled gently around her head. Renee's head grew hot. She tried not to appear as if she was interested in Delilah's body but didn't know how to do that. She *had* to look at her, so she furrowed her brow and tried to look pensive.

She stood near Delilah's face. "Are you okay?"

Delilah, hands folded on her stomach and feet crossed, wiggled her toes anxiously. "Yes. I'm a little nervous. It's not every day that I'm part of someone's art. A *naked* part of someone's art." She gave Renee a small smile, which she took to mean that Delilah was still willing.

"So, I'm going to take the various foods and place them on different parts of your body. Okay? Ready?"

Delilah nodded and stoically put her hands to her sides. "Ready."

Renee turned to the bowls and plates of food on the card table she'd set up next to the dining table and picked up the first bowl, containing macerated blackberries. She scooped some out and looked Delilah over. With a paintbrush, she made a circle on her stomach with vertical lines stemming out above and below the circle. To that, she added a splash of crimson from the bowl of red pepper puree.

One by one, she took each food and determined where and how it should be on Delilah's body.

The ripe white figs went perfectly between her breasts, and the honey dripping down along her ribcage made Delilah's nipples harden, which made Renee shiver. The caramel, still warm, awakened her skin with gooseflesh as Renee drizzled it back and forth all along her torso, making her look like a pastry.

The air became redolent of basil and cinnamon from infused chocolate ganache, which Renee spread on her lower belly.

"Oh, that smells so good," Delilah said, sniffing the air.

"I try to engage all the senses." She ran her fingers over Delilah's skin, pulling champagne slurry along. Delilah shivered.

"Are you cold?"

Delilah's cheeks flushed rosy. "No."

When she'd blanketed Delilah from head to toe with the sumptuous feast, Renee picked up her camera and said, "You are a smorgasbord."

Delilah smiled shyly and Renee watched as her skin raised with goosebumps. Then Renee began shooting. It was difficult keeping her eye in the viewfinder and not on the shimmering pomegranate seeds or peaches, glistening with their own cooked sugars, sliding in tiny increments, across Delilah's skin.

She shot from all sides, from above, individual body parts as well as the whole. Many shots later, she put the camera down.

"Well, that's it, I think. You must be stiff."

"A little." Delilah brought her knees up, making berry juice run down her thighs.

"I'll get some towels." Renee looked at the figs between Delilah's breasts. "What a shame to waste all this perfectly good food," she said with a chuckle.

"We don't have to waste it."

Renee's heart pounded. Was that an invitation? She reached for a fig, then pulled her hand back. Cautiously, she bent over and picked one up with her mouth. When her lips met Delilah's flesh, Delilah's stomach tightened. Renee felt as liquid as the nectar on Delilah's belly. With the fig still between her lips, she moved up to Delilah's face and touched the fig to her lips.

Delilah gently bit and gazed up at Renee, who bent again and kissed her. Delilah encouraged her with a hand. She loosened herself from Delilah's grip and pulled off her tee shirt and bra. She climbed on top of the table and lowered herself slowly onto Delilah, one leg between hers.

She licked caramel off her stomach, nibbled mango from her arms, and sucked the raspberry coulis that had settled on Delilah's fingers. Her shoulders, dusted in toasted coconut, were next, then the hollow of her throat, which cupped slivered almonds and pooled balsamic reduction. She kissed the taste of lavender on her neck.

Delilah writhed and arched beneath Renee's lips. The aroma of sweet sugars and fragrant herbs mingled with the scent of need.

Delilah tugged at Renee's pants and Renee obliged by removing them and her underwear and tossing them aside. She repositioned herself on Delilah and continued tasting the menu. She slowly slid her hand down her torso until she reached her thighs and slipped her fingers between them, making Delilah gasp.

She swirled a finger in the caramel and pulled some down where she could taste it and Delilah at the same time. One lick made Delilah moan. Renee continued licking, stopping now and then to add something else from the smorgasbord, as if they were condiments for Delilah's body. Renee had her tongue deep inside. Delilah tasted like ambrosia, and she knew that it wasn't the sweets.

Delilah's breathing was hard and ragged and she gripped Renee's shoulders. Renee, with her arms wrapped around her thighs, flattened her hands against Delilah's belly, smashing avocado and hazelnut-espresso mousse together in her fingers. Slippery, thick, and sticky, it echoed what was coating Renee's tongue. The sweet, salty, umami taste of Delilah intoxicated her even more as Delilah came on her tongue.

Delilah sat up, any semblance of design in the food completely eradicated. Colors and flavors were spread and combined all over her torso and limbs. She gently forced Renee into a sitting position and then straddled her so that they faced each other and their legs were intertwined. From her own torso, she gathered a combination of fruits and honey on her fingertip, and fed Renee the sweet mélange.

Renee bit gently down on Delilah's finger, startling her. But she didn't pull away. Instead, she pushed her finger in more, letting Renee stroke it with her lips. Delilah finally pulled her finger away and picked up a small paintbrush that Renee had left at her side and dipped it on herself, as if she were a palette of paints. A little red, a little blue, a little orange, she painted each of Renee's nipples with this mixture.

Renee closed her eyes and tilted her head up, savoring the delicious sensation. Then, Delilah's lips were on her neck, nibbling, and every nerve ending sparked, every part of her ached for release, like a pressure cooker left too long on the heat.

Delilah brought her hand down between Renee's legs and she was so wet that Delilah sank right in. Delilah kissed her as she stroked, and Renee became dizzy. She was shocked by a searing sensation on her clit, and she came hard.

Renee pushed herself up. Delilah's face was flushed and her eyes still glazed with her own orgasm. Her lips were bright red and Renee kissed her. She looked Delilah over. "I think you could use a shower."

"Think so?"

"Yes. Let me help you with that."

They both slid off the table and went to the bathroom.

After they'd showered, Delilah helped Renee clean up the dining room.

"We probably should've done this before showering," Delilah said.

Renee laughed. "Uh, yeah."

"Wanna grab something to eat?" Delilah asked.

"You're hungry?"

"I'm always hungry." Her voice and eyes told Renee that she wasn't just talking about food.

If life was a dish, soul was the inspiration, passion the recipe, and love the seasoning. The ingredients make it all worthwhile.

"Let's go," Renee said as she handed Delilah her jacket.

Delilah pulled her into another deep, long kiss.

"Planning any more projects?"

"Mmm, maybe," Delilah said with a grin. "Come on. I want to take you somewhere really special." And as they walked down the stairs, she took Renee's hand. "Did I mention that I really love food?"

ANGEL FOOD CAKE WITH MACERATED BLACKBERRIES AND BALSAMIC REDUCTION

Ingredients

2 pints blackberries, preferably organic

1/4 cup Amaretto

2 teaspoons sugar, preferably organic

1 teaspoon orange zest

1/2 cup good quality balsamic vinegar

1 (10- or 12-inch) angel food cake

Directions

1. Combine blackberries, Amaretto, sugar, and orange zest in a medium bowl. Let it sit at room temperature about 30 minutes, stirring it now and then.

2. Place vinegar in a small pot and bring to a boil; lower the heat to very low and simmer until the balsamic is reduced to half and is thick and syrupy. This will take about a half-hour, but check it occasionally. Let cool.

3. When you're ready to serve, slice the cake. On each slice, spoon some of the blackberries, then drizzle a little of the balsamic syrup over the top.

4. Eat it and love it. Use leftovers in sexy ways.

Makes 1 cake.

CRÈME BRÛLÉE

SACCHI GREEN

"HEY, RORY, SOMEBODY'S ASKING FOR you. Even knows your name."

I saw the sly grin on Audrey's face, saved my spreadsheet fast, and quit Excel. "I don't think it's a complaint or anything," she called to my retreating back.

I hadn't been focusing on the accounts anyway, just daydreaming. Remembering someone I'd never see again. Someone I didn't want to see because I wouldn't be able to resist her. The only person I'd met in years who could make me melt inside the shell I'd constructed so carefully, and then break right on through it. It had been just that one night, around this time last year…

And there was Raf, in the very solid flesh, seated in the same alcove overlooking the salt marsh. I could feel her presence all the way across the dining room. Last year, I'd bribed Audrey to let me wait on that table. This time I didn't even bother to snatch her apron and order pad.

The broad back and granite-gray hair clipped short could have belonged to any of thousands of guys vacationing on Cape Cod. Or hundreds of women, for that matter, being this close to Provincetown. But I knew exactly who it was. Knew every line and curve and hollow of the body beneath the slate blue jacket and white shirt, not to mention the gray slacks. I'd explored all of her well enough to make sketches from memory, and to chisel and polish her image out of pink Cadillac Mountain granite from Maine.

"Good evening," I said as demurely as I could manage, just as I had the first time. "I'm Rory. I'll be serving you tonight."

Raf kept her gaze on the menu spread out across the white tablecloth, but her mouth twitched and then expanded into a wide grin. "I'll have my usual," she said, and lifted those clear hazel eyes to me. I could barely keep my own lips steady.

"Two appetizers to share? Wellfleet oysters on the half-shell and ceviche of Chatham scallops?" I looked pointedly at the empty chair across from her. A year ago it had been nicely filled indeed by a voluptuous young thing trying to obey her dyke Daddy's instructions to eat the raw shellfish whether she wanted to or not. I'd taken pity and told the girl that the lime juice in the ceviche more or less "cooks" the scallops. "And two entrées, the bouillabaisse, and the cioppino? With the house White Zinfandel, black coffee, no dessert?" I'd be damned if I'd ask where the girl was. Not yet, at least. What was her name? Juliana?

"Actually, I was kind of looking forward to dessert."

My blood had already been simmering. Now it came to a slow boil, remembering how we'd gone at each other like starving wildcats in my studio at 2 a.m. when Juliana was safely asleep at their motel, exhausted after an evening of clubbing in Provincetown.

"But for the rest," Raf went on, "just one appetizer and entrée, unless I can get you to share with me. Would your boss allow that?"

"I'm the boss tonight. Technically, the assistant manager." Which didn't guarantee that I'd get away with it. Audrey could be bribed, but there were six other waitresses, already intensely interested in what I was up to. Tough. It wouldn't be easy to replace an assistant manager who also did the accounting. Not this late in the season. "And as the boss, I happen to know that the duck in beach plum-Cabernet sauce is especially good tonight. I'll go for the oysters, but duck instead of bouillabaisse." Raf already knew that I'm far from the submissive type, but the emphasis on choosing my own meal wouldn't hurt.

I sat down, caught Audrey's eye, and motioned her to the table to take our order. Then I swept the room with a steely gaze that got the rest of the waitresses hustling the way they were supposed to.

"I went by your studio and the gallery," Raf said, as soon as we'd been supplied with ice water and lemon slices. "I was hoping you'd be there, covered in clay dust like you were last summer."

Daddy and girl had wandered from the co-op gallery into my studio, clearly looking for a corner just secluded enough to pretend no one could see them making out. The girl's shorts had been so brief they revealed rosy traces of the proprietary barcode Daddy's hand had imprinted on her naughty ass. They must have indulged in a bit of after-lunch action before taking a stroll through the galleries.

Juliana had pouted when they'd seen me there, but Raf had chatted, admired my stone and porcelain nudes, stroked a tempting set of smooth marble buttocks, and probed a big finger down between the irresistible thighs. My crotch got wet enough to dampen the clay dust layering my jeans.

When they turned up later at the restaurant where I work to earn the minimal living that art can't provide, it felt like the truck that had hit me had stopped to take me for a ride.

The way Raf looked at me now in my conservative pants suit made me sure she was thinking more about how I'd looked later that night covered in nothing at all. Just the way I was remembering her.

"I've been working more in stone than clay since then. Still get covered in dust, though."

"I noticed some of your new sculptures, there and in that fancier gallery up the hill." She hesitated. "That piece in the pink-speckled stone, with the 'Not for Sale' sign." Her sun-ruddy face got a little redder. She would never have seen herself from just the angle I'd portrayed. Rear view, recumbent, about quarter-scale and nude, of course, with smooth flesh emerging out of a jagged granite base. Broad shoulders, the side-swell of a breast, head turned to the right, just a few details of face and brush-cut hair...the effect was on the verge of being abstract, but clearly inspired by a real person. And she knew it.

"That's brought me a couple of commissions," I said, with studied casualness. "Thanks for the inspiration. Who'd have thought that anyone rich enough to afford it would want a stylized portrait of her lover in stone? Or that the subject would be willing to pose for my sketches? Maybe I'll be able to make a living with my art one of these days after all."

The oysters arrived just in time to save Raf from having to figure out what to say. I enjoyed the hell out of her discombobulation. Let her wonder whether I'd been using her just for my own artistic purposes, even if I couldn't deceive myself.

I still blurted out, "But I'll never sell that one." So much for staying cool and detached.

"I'm glad." Raf plucked an oyster on its half-shell from the bed of ice chips and raised it toward me like a salute before tilting the sweet juice into her mouth. I did the same. We managed a simultaneous sliding of the oysters themselves across our tongues and down our throats, swallowing in perfect synchronization, then licking our lips. And grinning.

"The sauce is worth trying, too." I spooned a bit of chipotle mignonette onto another oyster, then licked it slowly off before sucking the slippery morsel into my mouth.

"Mmm." Raf tried it, even more dramatic in her licking and sucking. "Not bad, but not the very best sauce I've ever tasted."

A sound at my shoulder like stifled laughter erupted into a snort. Audrey, bringing the scallops ceviche in their little avocado boat. I pretended not to have heard. As soon as she was gone Raf raised a questioning eyebrow and jerked her head in the direction of Audrey's sashaying butt.

I raised my hands in exasperation and shook my head. "Audrey's a good kid in her way, but a one-trick pony, and that trick is getting her posterior paddled by any means necessary. Once in a while I'll indulge her, but I make her earn it. Last time you were here that's how I bribed her to let me wait on your table. There's nothing more between us."

We finished off the last two oysters sedately, though we were close to laughter, before turning to the contrast of tender scallops tangy with lime and jalapeño and the buttery luxury of perfectly ripened avocado. I could almost forget the memory of young Juliana sampling the same dish with a high degree of suspicion.

Raf must have been thinking of Juliana, too, or maybe she read my mind. "Funny how much better food tastes when you're with someone who really knows how to enjoy it."

I still wouldn't ask what had become of the girl. "Maybe we should have ordered lobster, too, for the full Tom Jones effect."

"That's exactly it! When I said something along those lines to Juliana, she had no idea what I was talking about. Never heard of Tom Jones the movie, much less the book, or even the singer."

"Ah, youth," I said. "Just the same, she's certainly a tasty bit of arm candy for a stroll around Provincetown."

"She was, wasn't she?"

Past tense. So my first unasked question was answered.

And then the second.

"We outgrew each other. At least I outgrew her, and she transferred to a West Coast college." She shrugged. "It was about time."

The intensity in her hazel eyes as she watched for my reaction was my cue to ask what it was time for now. A second frantic, earth-shaking fuck with me, and then on to the next sweet young morsel who wanted to act out fantasies of submission with the biggest, baddest gray-fox butch around? The fuck I would make sure of. The rest I'd just as soon skip.

The entrées arrived just in time to save me from having to respond. "It's not too late to add some lobster," I said.

Raf grinned but shook her head. "Better not bite off more than we can chew." She plucked a mussel from the cioppino tureen, yanked open its shell with her fingers, and ran her tongue around the interior. I joined in the game with a quick twist to tear duck leg from duck thigh, brandishing the drumstick at her before sinking my teeth into the meatiest part. Purple plum sauce ran down my chin and hand.

"How about a baby calamari?" She held one out on her fork and made the tentacles seem to dance in the air. I almost wished Juliana had been there after all so I could watch her reaction.

"Aw, how cute." I held out the duck leg with the bite I'd taken out of it uppermost. "Slip it right into there." The tiny cephalopod made it from fork to drumstick to my mouth. It went as well with my plum sauce and pecan pilaf side dish as it would have with the cioppino broth.

Even in the alcove, we weren't all that secluded. Several nearby observers were taking an interest in our antics, so we toned it down a bit and concentrated more seriously on our food.

All this time I'd stayed aware of what went on in the dining room and in the bar beyond. Customers waiting for tables were bunching up in the bar, so I excused myself for a few minutes. I licked sauce off my fingers, left purple streaks across the white linen napkin, and went to straighten things out. An annex usually reserved for small private parties was opened up, tables were set, and the stand-by waitress helping out at the bar was assigned to cover them. I went back to Raf.

"Doesn't look like you'll be getting off early tonight," she observed, and took a sip of wine.

"Not unless I want to settle for a quickie in the ladies' room, which I don't. The pink and powder blue décor does nothing for me."

Raf nearly choked on the wine. I thought for a few seconds that I might need to demonstrate my Heimlich maneuver skills. The prospect of squeezing my arms around her from behind had a certain carnal attraction, but she recovered soon enough and mopped her face with her napkin, only slightly spotted with tomato sauce from the cioppino.

"Well then," she said after drawing a few deep breaths, "when *do* you expect to get out of work? In time for a jaunt into P-town? Or maybe a walk on some beach?"

I opened my eyes wide in mock astonishment. "You mean, like, a real date?"

Raf didn't miss a beat. "Nothing wrong with a change of pace now and then."

"You have a point, there. I moved to Wellfleet to leave behind the distractions of P-town-and-Gomorrah and focus on my art, but it might be fun to stroll along Commercial Street with the brand of arm candy that gives all the baby-femmes wet dreams."

"I'm sure you inspire plenty of wet dreams yourself." The look in her eyes would have made her meaning clear even if she hadn't laid her big hand over mine on the table.

"There's a pretty good market among the young set for weathered androgyny like mine, too," I conceded, staying deliberately casual but not withdrawing my hand. "Especially if I make an effort to look extra mean and tough. But it was getting to be more trouble than it was worth."

"I know just what you mean." She drew her hand back and finished off her wine. "So how about we try the old-fashioned way and get to know each other. You close here when? Ten o'clock?"

"Nine. Wellfleet doesn't keep Provincetown hours. Where should I pick you up? If we meet at my studio we might not get any farther."

She told me where she was staying, we finished off what food we felt like bothering with, and I got back to managing the increasingly busy restaurant. Just before nine, I slipped into the kitchen, wheedled the cook into letting me take two special desserts in their white pottery ramekins and a container of ice to keep them chilled. The bartender, who owed me several favors, agreed to handle closing up.

On the long stretch from Wellfleet through Truro to Provincetown, Raf and I chatted like blind dates feeling each other out, while repressing the urge to feel each other up.

"What made you decide to be a sculptor? Especially with stone?"

"Oh, I started out with clay pots, mugs, that sort of thing. Pretty commercial. There's a good market for crafts in tourist season. But stone…maybe it's the challenge. To feel the shape a piece could have, and then to cut and chisel and grind and polish until, by my own strength and sweat and profanity, I get the right balance between what I wanted and what the stone can take. When it really works out, which isn't a sure bet, there's a rush like nothing else."

Raf started to speak, paused, then came out with it. "Sounds like the mother of all power trips."

"Oh, yeah." I wasn't offended. "And the best thing about stone is that it's solid. Cut or bore or chisel into it, and it's stone all the way down. You need to recognize the grain, and sometimes striations, but there's no soft core with chaotic feelings or longings or resentments." Maybe I was revealing too much. Maybe I wanted to.

"Looks like you almost always choose to sculpt naked women. Or just parts of them." Raf wasn't pulling any punches either.

"Is there any sculptor who doesn't? And they sell."

"Yours are something special. And you don't always sell them. Do you...well, do you use many models?"

"Can't usually afford models. But I have an excellent memory." Enough of that. "So how about you? What do you do besides instruct young beauties in the finer points of sex and submission?"

Raf hesitated. "You know what? Let's skip the P-town scene and go walk and talk on a beach."

So we didn't make it to the bars and crowds after all. From Pilgrim Heights, where Route 6 starts downhill, the bright lights along the hook-shaped shore of Provincetown made a pattern so lovely it was better not to spoil it by getting too close. Instead, we veered off toward Race Point, where we walked barefoot on the sand by moonlight, watching waves roll slowly in under starry skies. This was as clichéd as it gets, and it was too windy for much conversation but exhilarating. It was good to be sharing something exhilarating besides sex.

Eventually, we found a slightly sheltered spot in the dunes. The waves were out of sight, but we could still hear them, and the stars looked even brighter as the moon sank lower.

Raf settled her butt into the sand and began to talk. "I work as a supervisor for the Post Office, currently in central Vermont. Nice country, but kind of isolated in many ways." She paused.

"I know the quarries up around there," I said, to fill the silence. "Some of the best marble in the world. I can't afford the perfect stuff, but I go there to look for remnants of broken slabs or pieces with faults. I like the challenge of making the imperfect stones into something special."

"Hey, that's great! Call me next time you're heading that way. Stay with me. I mean—I don't want to lose you this time."

It was too dark to be sure, but I had the impression that she was blushing. Then she went on. "There are quite a few married dykes in Vermont trying to make it in farming or arts and crafts. At least Boston is within reach. My ex and I broke up when we both felt like we'd become different people."

I put a not-quite-comradely arm around her solid back. "Yeah, I know how those things go."

Raf followed my comradely arm routine. We wriggled even closer to each other. "There's a club in Boston, women-only BDSM."

"Yeah, I've heard of it." I mentioned the name. "I know a couple of the founders, but they drifted away when the members got too involved in wrangling about bylaws and business meetings and so forth. "

"Well, that's where I found out that old-school butches of a certain age were back in style. Or maybe they never went out of style in the city. Whatever, the youngsters were lining up for some good old-fashioned domination, and giving them what they wanted came naturally to me. It was great, for quite a while. Intoxicating."

"Was?" No guarantee needed. I just wondered.

"Maybe. I don't know. It gets to be so much work, fulfilling their fantasies, being who they want me to be, not getting—not getting what you and I had last year. I couldn't get you out of my mind."

"My mind isn't the only place that remembers you." I slid my hand along her thigh. Cocksure or, as now, on the verge of vulnerable, Raf still had that aura, that presence, whatever it was that grabbed me so hard and made my depths clench. She turned, enveloped me in those strong arms…and an arc of headlights swept across the top of the dune and skimmed her gray hair. New arrivals, and from the sounds, they weren't here just to stay in their car and make out.

I sighed, then sighed again more deeply, enjoying the way the motion rubbed my breasts against her chest.

"Maybe we're too mature to roll around in the sand here, anyway," she said.

"I guess. Just like we're mature enough to get the most out of playing with our food." I tried to get disentangled. "Come on back to the car. I brought dessert."

Raf's hand cupped my ass to help me up. "But I thought you were going to be my dessert!"

"That'll be second dessert. And maybe again for first breakfast. This is different."

The newcomers seemed to be busy building a fire of driftwood on the beach. I moved my car to the far end of the parking lot. In the glow of the overhead light I leaned over the front seat into the back to get my treasures out of their chilly container. Raf took the opportunity to knead my upturned butt and tease between my thighs, but with a steel-willed effort I got the ramekins safely onto a towel folded on the front seat between us.

"Crème brûlée!" I said triumphantly. "Have you ever had it?"

"Just seen it on restaurant menus a time or two without paying attention. What's it mean? Bruised cream?"

"That sounds intriguingly kinky, but no. More like broiled cream. The top is covered with raw sugar, melted under a broiler or a propane torch, and then it hardens like glass." I dug some plastic spoons out of the side pocket on the door where I tend to shove them when I get drive-through coffee.

"Dig in," I said, knowing what would be likely to happen. Raf's spoon broke on the mottled golden surface.

"You're the stonecutter in this crew," she said. "You do it."

I took out my pocketknife, covered it in plastic wrap that had protected the desserts, and brought it down hard on one sugar-glazed portion. Cracks rayed out, letting glimpses of the inner custard showed through. "That's yours. Now you break my shell."

She did it with one hand, while the other pulled my head close for a long, sensuous kiss. Finally, she pulled away. "So did I break through?"

I couldn't even remember whether we'd done anything as slow and sweet as kissing last year. "Oh, yeah." I was breathless. "No shell left at all."

"Looks like some crunchy bits left in the dishes." She took my spoon and scooped up some of the rich creamy custard along with fragments of sugar glaze. "Mmm. Now I know what you see in this. Such rich, smooth cream inside that stony exterior." She took another bite, then offered me one. We alternated with the spoon, feeding each other, until the last bites were accidentally-on-purpose smeared across our lips. The licking and kissing that followed got us so revved up that driving all the way back to Wellfleet without relief was out of the question, so I pulled off at the Pilgrim Springs Trail parking lot, mercifully unoccupied.

This time, I won the race to get each other's clothes off. My wiry build let me twist and wriggle around more, so I had her chest binding loosened and my hands full of breasts rejoicing in their freedom before she got under my sports bra. She chewed her way down my neck and shoulder and made me arch backward when her mouth got to my small breasts, even as I was working my hand under her loosened belt and into the warm, pungent mysteries below.

We were still too cramped in the car for all we needed. It's a good thing the National Seashore provides sturdy picnic tables. I feasted first, kneeling on pine needles while Raf leaned back against the table. I got her slacks down far enough that I could feel the coppery bush I remembered, even if there was no telling in the dark whether it was still untouched by gray. All that mattered was the creamy tang on her full lips, the tension of her straining clit when my tongue lashed at it, the clenching of her muscles around my fingers deep inside her and the full-throated cry that came when her spasms of release shook the wooden boards so hard they creaked.

Then it was my turn to press my naked ass against the hard-edged table while Raf's strong hands pinched and kneaded and made all my tenderest parts quiver with pleasure close to pain. At last I moaned, "Inside! Deep!" and when she obliged, my hips tilted to meet the pressure, demanded more pressure, and I rode her hand until stars exploded out of my center to hang in the night sky above me, brighter than all the galaxies in the distant Milky Way.

For all that, we were more than ready to start over when we made it back to Wellfleet. "I don't actually live at my studio," I told Raf. "I have a perfectly good bedroom in a little saltbox house down the road." But she voted for the studio again, out of nostalgia, so we rolled out my old futon there and went at it as though our two bodies needed to consume each other, driven by a common weight of life, of pleasure and pain, of hurling our joy against time's wall.

This time she didn't have to leave at sunrise. "This must be, what, fourth dessert? Or first breakfast?"

I stretched a bit stiffly and rubbed against her. She seemed to have acquired a scratch mark or two on her flanks where I sleepily recalled gripping her hard in extremity. "I'm not sure, but it won't be long before 'bruised cream' is the right term after all. And that's just fine with me."

Things had never been finer, in fact. I felt another sculpture coming on, in creamy marble this time, with maybe a few small faults along its sides for added interest.

CRÈME BRÛLÉE

Ingredients

2 1/2 cups heavy cream

1 teaspoon vanilla extract

8 egg yolks

1/4 cup + 2 tablespoons granulated white sugar

1/4 cup brown sugar

Directions

1. Preheat oven to 300 degrees F.

2. In a saucepan, bring cream and vanilla to a simmer (do not boil!) and remove from heat.

3. In a large bowl, whisk together egg yolks and white sugar until thick and smooth. Add cream, a little at a time, and whisk in until well blended.

4. Pour mixture evenly into 6 ramekins. Place ramekins in a baking dish and fill dish with water until it comes halfway up sides of ramekins. Bake until set around edges, but still jiggly in center, about 45 to 50 minutes. Remove from oven and water bath. Refrigerate for at least 2 hours or overnight.

5. When ready to serve, sprinkle equal amounts of brown sugar over each one. Use a hand torch to brown the tops, or place ramekins under the broiler until sugar melts.

Makes **6.**

TURN THE TABLES

YVONNE HEIDT

LEONITA RAISED HER DRIPPING SWORD, pointed it to the stands, and screamed her victory into the sky. The noise of the cheering crowd echoed around the arena and created a vocal thunderstorm of adulation.

Lio-Ness!

Lio-Ness!

She lowered her gaze to stare at the Governor until he nodded slightly, giving her permission to leave now that the man's body lay lifeless at her feet. Leonita saluted him, then walked back across the bloody sands, leaving the stench of death and fear behind her.

The spectators threw flowers into her path. As they should, she thought. She'd given them a battle they'd remember. A fight so vicious that it stirred even the most jaded of them.

She stopped at the gate, turned and raised her arms once more, and the volume of the crowd's frenzied storm of exaltation increased.

Once inside the tunnels, she let her posture relax slightly. The fight promoter slapped her on the back, clearly enthused by her win, and the coin that lined his purse because of it.

She refrained from snarling at him only because he handed her a leather bag that contained her own winnings, along with her meager belongings.

She could tell by the hatred in their expressions which trainers had bet against her, and put their money on the male barbarian, but it was no longer any of her concern what these men did.

Leonita continued to walk past the caged beasts, unfortunate prisoners, slaves, and the physician's enclave. The guards waved her by as she climbed the steep stairs. She stopped and murmured a plea to her personal goddess before she opened the door.

If all was well, the means to her freedom would be right outside in a mule-drawn carriage that would take her away from the crowds still screaming for blood and gore, the slavers, pimps, and power-hungry politicians. The way out provided by The Lioness's benefactress, who pledged to her a house, far, far from this *civilized* city.

She took a deep breath, opened the door, and saw the promise fulfilled, waiting on the dusty road. Leonita exhaled with relief, and climbed into the luxurious cart.

The driver had already been arranged and paid for. Leonita wearily leaned back, adjusting her body to minimize the pain of her wounds during the ride on the long, winding road to the palace.

Flavia had used the blistering summer heat as an excuse to leave their box at the arena. She knew she needn't bother, but chose to be polite. Her husband, Paulus the Governor, oversaw the games and cared little what she did, as long as she kept her duties impeccable as his wife in and around the political forum. He had no real power over her, and he knew it. Flavia's father was a powerful man, one that Paulus knew better than to anger.

She also knew he was aware of Flavia's proclivities toward female slaves. It was a secret they both kept well, as he had some secrets of his own. The marriage of convenience worked for both of them, and as long as she was discreet, she could play all she desired.

And what she desired was The Lioness.

Flavia had rushed back to her palace, and the farewell party she'd arranged. She tested the water in the sunken pool to assess the heat, sampled the feast waiting to be served, and then re-issued orders to her personal slaves, Xanthia and Tasia.

The Lioness's arrival caused a commotion at the entrance to her private quarters. Flavia set aside the dignity she carried as her social standing and wealth demanded, picked up her long skirt, and ran for the door.

"Oh," She stopped abruptly. "You're filthy and bloody."

"Forgive me, *Domina*. Because of your generosity, I am a slave no longer, and the women who used to prepare me for you are now denied to me. I came straight from the sands."

Flavia smiled, but gathered her white dress closer to her body. "By the Gods, you were magnificent, Lioness!"

"Leonita. I left The Lioness in the arena."

"How much of that blood is yours?" Flavia asked. Small rivers, the color of rust, trailed down Leonita's hard-packed body. Her long, dark hair was snarled and dirty with it, and her sandals left muddy footprints on the spotless stone floor.

"Truly, I know not."

Flavia rang a bell and her personal slaves appeared at once. Two beautiful, matching blonde women who resembled each other so much they may have been identical twins. Slaves who knew her most intimate desires, but possessed little of the challenge and bold thrill that bedding the warrior presented.

The first time she saw The Lioness in the arena, Flavia became obsessed with her. She *had* to have her, but she'd found that even a Roman woman of the highest standing could and would be told no. It nearly drove her to madness when she had to settle for purchasing Leonita's time from the dirty, low-bred *lanista* who owned her. With each of her victories, Leonita's intimate time and purchase price for freedom increased, and it had taken Flavia months to persuade him to sell. A feat accomplished only by a few choice, well-placed words to her husband, who threatened to ruin the man if he did not acquiesce to Flavia's desire.

Of course, after pocketing the small fortune she'd given him, the snake arranged and promoted a match against the male barbarian in order to make the most money before he lost his star attraction. Flavia would have loved to see the expression on his smarmy, oily face when The Lioness won.

Still, she thought, even with The Lioness's excellent fighting skills, it could have gone the other way, and she would have lost her forever. It was a little surprising to her that the loss of her lover would have been greater than the loss of money to Flavia. It was one thing to have bought a gladiatrix's time, and another to want her as an equal, to crave her companionship as well as her body.

Flavia turned to the slaves. "Tasia, Xanthia. Undress her, she needs a bath."

"Yes, *Domina*," they answered in unison.

Leonita towered above the smaller women, necessitating Tasia to fetch a small stool to unfasten the leather straps across her chest and shoulders and drop the heavy, bloody harness on the floor. Xanthia unbuckled the short leather and chain mail skirt, revealing the only place on her body that wasn't covered in dirt and gore.

Naked, The Lioness rivaled any of the perfectly carved statues gracing Flavia's household. Leonita licked her lips, and stared unashamed into Flavia's eyes.

The bold challenge caused her heart to flutter. Flavia spoke past the lump in her throat. "Tasia, Xanthia, join her, please."

They untied the halters of the other's simple shifts, and both dresses fell silently around their ankles. Each took one of Leonita's hands, and they went down the marble steps together. Flavia reclined luxuriously on the couch next to the pool to watch.

The water turned muddy and red before being flushed by the pool's intricate pipe system. Leonita dived repeatedly to soak the grime from her body, and wet her hair. Several cuts and abrasions began burning, but she ignored them. They would heal soon enough. Her wounded spirit would take much, much longer.

The steam rose from the baths while the scents of expensive oils and soaps filled the bathing area. Tasia and Xanthia washed Leonita's hair, generously lathering the suds and massaging her scalp. They playfully ducked her when they were finished.

Sleek and slippery, they twisted and turned under the water, taking every opportunity to brush their naked bodies against hers. They gasped, and then giggled when she returned the favors, quick caresses in soft places before they darted away again.

Leonita had known carnal pleasure with them previously. With their permission she'd enjoyed the unexpected gift of their time from Flavia after one of her matches in the arena. By the time she left, the women had been exhausted from her attentions, and she herself had been happily sated.

After she'd been thoroughly bathed, Leonita returned to the shallow side, where Flavia waited, and watched her with eyes full of desire. What had the wife of a Roman Senator seen in her? Leonita knew her physique was powerful, well sculpted, and strong. It had to be—the months and years of training saw to that. She was aware of the scars that covered her body, both from fighting and the sadistic trainers that took pleasure in whipping the slaves in their charge. Yet, Flavia bought her body, time and again. Not to hurt, but to worship. It was a strange feeling, and when it came to Flavia, Leonita was perpetually in emotional turmoil.

The stark contrast between her plump soft curves versus her slave companions in the *ludus*, was evident in the tough battle-scarred women she'd willingly slept with over the years. Leonita would never deny that as The Lioness, she often sought the rough, fast, and furious couplings after vicious battles. It was a way to release the adrenaline, to come down after the fights.

That sex was far different and further from these opulent rooms than the moon. For The Lioness, it was as much about maintaining dominance as their leader within the group. She hadn't needed love. There was no place for tenderness in the arena or the *ludus*. Kindness would always be perceived as weakness, and used against you to keep you in check.

Flavia watched Leonita walk out of the bath. The water dripping from her hair ran down her naked torso. Her body, scarred and sculpted by the regimented training of a celebrated gladiatrix, contrasted with the soft, pink flesh at the apex of her thighs. Flavia was again aware of the tightening in her throat that made speech difficult. It seemed to her as if the Goddess of War, Bellona, emerged and approached her.

"Come," Leonita said and extended her hand down to help Flavia up from her seated position. She felt weak inside but took it, feeling the brush of The Lioness's scars and rough callouses against her palm.

A tiny shiver of apprehension ran along her spine. Leonita, as a slave, had been obligated to obey Flavia. She had no choice. But now, here she stood, taller than her husband, stronger than the pampered men in her world, and as a free woman.

Her knees went weak, and she slightly stumbled. Might she be in danger? Once she asked herself the question, it took her several moments to arrest the apprehension that followed. Flavia straightened her spine and dismissed the trepidation. She stepped back to allow Tasia to dry Leonita with fluffy towels made of the finest Egyptian cotton.

Xanthia returned and led Flavia through the arched doorway, into the dining room, and away from the heat of the bath chamber. She'd fasted all this day in anticipation of the feast of food and flesh. The tables were laden with rich food and wine, the best that could be imported from the provinces that Rome controlled. Flavia had put a good deal of effort and money into this celebration.

Before Flavia reached her couch, Leonita stayed her with a firm hand on her shoulder. She'd refused the clothing Xanthia offered, and so stood pressed against Flavia's back, completely naked, emanating heat and fresh scent from the bath.

In the time it took her to blink, her gown was on the floor. Flavia gasped and attempted to unsuccessfully cover herself. For Flavia to touch any slave was her right as a mistress. To *be* touched without permission was punishable by death.

But, by Flavia's own signature, The Lioness was a slave no longer. When she had requested Leonita attend her tonight, she thought it would be a farewell dinner, gratitude for the freedom she'd purchased for her. That Leonita wanted Flavia of her own will, and not because she felt obligated to perform, was unexpected. Or did she hate her for the time she was required to spend with Flavia previously? Did The Lioness want revenge?

"Am I on the menu tonight, or are you?" Leonita's hands gripped Flavia's waist, pulling her back, rolling her naked vulva against Flavia's bare ass.

The return of apprehension raised the hair on the back of Flavia's neck, and she shivered with fear. Hot breath exhaled near her ear, followed by a nip of sharp teeth. It was horrifying, it was delicious, and her knees gave way again.

"No!" Flavia said. The act reminded her of her husband as he took her roughly from behind in the dark, with no regard for anything other than the need for heirs. Then he would give his love to his own bed-slave in the Senator's chambers. She hated this position, she felt humiliated.

"Shh," The Lioness whispered. "I know."

Flavia tensed as The Lioness continued to mimic the fornication act, rolling her hips against her, but Leonita continued the hushing sound whispered into her ear until it became invasive, the imagined vibration raced along Flavia's skin, traveled to her breasts then straight to her inner core. Flavia was taken aback to find when her thighs rubbed together, they were slippery. Always, she'd done the touching, the worshiping of Leonita's glorious body. Now the tables were turned, and Leonita's wet labia rubbing against her, stroking between her buttocks and sliding against Flavia's most sensitive flesh was near maddening. She attempted to take a step forward, and Leonita's fingers tightened, curled into her flesh, holding her in place while she continued her intimate act. She felt the sharp nip of teeth on her shoulder and shivered.

Flavia was frightened, she was excited. Pressure built in her clit until it throbbed in time with her heart and her breathing became labored. She struggled little when Leonita easily picked her up, and laid her on the dining couch. She fought to hold herself still, to not place her hand between her own thighs to complete her climax, or order Xanthia to do so.

"Still not the real you." Leonita reached into Flavia's hair, and removed the pins holding it in the elaborate style. Though Flavia's long curls fell about her shoulders and over her breasts, somehow it also managed to make her feel more exposed.

"Much better," The Lioness said. "Prettier, softer."

Leonita watched Flavia smile slowly, and she felt her knees weaken. Not from fear—she feared nothing—but because Flavia, a woman of means and power, chose her to give herself to. She hadn't objected, or ordered her away. Leonita had felt her unease, but also knew it had turned to desire.

For her.

Where there had only been whips, sticks, and brutal beatings to subdue her, Flavia had conquered her with gentle touches and soft kisses. She felt a fierce protectiveness toward her. Leonita arranged herself next to Flavia on the couch and entwined her leg over her smaller ones, shifting position until Flavia's head lay on her shoulder and Leonita could easily glance down at her fine features.

Flavia rearranged her long tresses so that they covered Leonita's scarred stomach, and the soft hair tickled the skin on her hips. When Leonita sensed she was about to speak, she plucked a wine-soaked pear from the platter Tasia held, and instead pressed it against Flavia's lips, and watched as wine dribbled down her chin and pooled in the delicate hollow of her throat.

"Here," Leonita said. "Let me help you." She bent her head down, and took a bite from the other side. The flesh of the fruit was of the perfect texture, and the expensive wine tingled against her tongue. Between the two of them, they nibbled until only the core was between their lips, and Leonita tossed it over her shoulder.

She didn't know which of the rich foods she should choose next. The fare was far different than she was used to and the smells intoxicated her nearly as much as Flavia's heat. Her stomach grumbled, and Flavia laughed.

"Here," she said. "Let me help you this time." Flavia sat up, and curled her legs to the side, her full breasts dangling dangerously close to Leonita's lips while she still reclined. She caressed the side of one breast softly with the back of her hand before she enveloped it in her palm and pulled Flavia closer. Leonita nipped her, then sucked Flavia's large areole, rolling her tongue across her hardened nipple, and attempted to draw as much of her breast into her mouth as she could.

Flavia sighed and rubbed her thighs together, but stopped Leonita's hand when she tried to part her legs. She leaned back, and away from her. "No, let me." She took another fruit from the silver tray. "Try this." She held the half fig in the palm of her hand, baked and garnished with cream, and offered it to her, then took one for herself.

"It resembles a woman's cunt."

Flavia blushed at Leonita's crass word, but she wasn't going to flower her statement. A rose was a rose, after all.

Flavia slowly extended her tongue, curling it seductively and sliding it along the slit of the fig, leaving a trail of cream around her mouth. The sight sent a ghostly stroke along Leonita's own folds, the echo of what Flavia was doing to that fig opened her memory of how it felt to have Flavia take her to a screaming climax with her mouth, bringing the warrior to her knees and helpless in the face of her desire. She ate her own fig quickly without tasting it.

But Flavia would have none of it. She demanded the need for food be satisfied first, and insisted that desire and hunger were related. Both should be drawn out deliciously, until one was full and sated. She gave Leonita another fig. "Slowly."

Tasia came next with a platter of meat, filled with assorted beef, pork, and lamb. She kneeled next to the couch while Leonita and Flavia fed each other bite-sized morsels, then licked each other's fingers clean of the juices.

Xanthia tipped a shell against Leonita's lips and the motion rolled an oyster into her mouth. The slippery texture, the buttery taste against her tongue, reminded her of a woman's intimate flesh. She was beginning to appreciate the seduction of food, the foreplay of it.

Leonita couldn't take her eyes off of Flavia's mouth, the way her lips pursed around the meat, the quick glance of her sharp little teeth as she chewed, the seductive way she licked her lips, and her soft smiles between each bite. Each course brought its own torture to her, and she was finding it increasingly difficult to continue to eat. The growl began low in her throat. She knocked the tray from Tasia's hand, and reached to grab Flavia, to shove her down on the couch and take her, possess her, fuck her until they both screamed with release. But Flavia was much faster than she looked, and easily got to her feet to evade her.

"Shh." Flavia whispered. "Soon." She motioned for Xanthia to bring another, smaller tray. While she waited, she gave Leonita some more wine, which she drank greedily. Her stomach was full, the day and battle were weak upon her now, and she had little energy to chase her. She was frustrated, but not tired. Her cunt ached and throbbed with unanswered lust.

"Is the Lioness sated?" Flavia asked.

"Please, Flavia. No more teasing. I am on fire. There is but one thirst left to conquer tonight."

Flavia was taken aback by the simplistic, quiet tone of Leonita's statement. She used to enjoy making her beg for release, found a thrill in conquering the warrior. Just this moment, she didn't feel that way at all.

She put down the wine. "What is it you desire? Tell me."

"I wish to taste you, to worship you until your desire becomes so great, it will fill my mouth with the very essence of your spirit that I will swallow and take with me always." Leonita pointed to her heart. "Here, I will carry you here."

The soft words carried strong emotion and Flavia's heart seemed to stutter before resuming its normal pace.

They had no future together as a couple, she knew that. She had no real rights other than those from her father, first, and then her husband. She was fortunate that her husband was kinder than most, and had secrets he didn't want out. But he would never entertain her wish to move to the coast with Leonita. Perhaps he would allow her to go when his political career was over.

But now was not the time to entertain these impossible thoughts. It was better to let The Lioness leave without her. At least now, she didn't have to worry that she would die in the cruel and bloody sands of the arena for the entertainment of others. Flavia had the rest of the night with her and she didn't intend to waste it.

"Come here, Flavia." Leonita held her hands out.

Flavia straddled her on the couch to wrap her arms around Leonita's broad shoulders before kissing her deeply, passionately. She was so lost in the moment that when Leonita abruptly ended the kiss and slid down between Flavia's legs until her knees were braced on the floor, it took her by surprise. Flavia was now straddling Leonita's head and she nearly lost her balance, but Leonita braced her buttocks with her hands before she could fall.

Leonita's first soft kisses on Flavia's clitoris were both gentle and playful. Flavia placed her hands on the back of the couch and tilted her hips closer and she watched Leonita's tongue as she licked her. The sight was incredibly erotic, and she instantly heated from the inside out, rocking herself gently with the slow rhythm of Leonita's pace, floating along with the leisurely building pressure of the orgasms that were being created.

She trembled and cried out from the sharp nip of Leonita's teeth, and the vibration of her moans against her flesh. She looked over her shoulder and glimpsed Xanthia's head between Leonita's thighs, her long hair to the side, and Flavia instantly felt her body respond, and felt Leonita greedily lapping at her, which only brought more.

Tasia appeared in front of Flavia to caress her breasts. Flavia pulled her hair and kissed her, using her tongue to fuck her mouth the way she was being fucked. Her nipples hardened when Tasia twisted them the way Flavia loved, the pain that connected to her core, spurring the pace.

She ached, she shook, but there was that part of her that held back from letting herself go completely. She didn't like not being in control, but when she attempted to pull back from Leonita's mouth, Leonita gripped her ass harder, forcing her closer. Flavia took one of Tasia's hands from her breast and directed her to play with herself.

Flavia panted against Tasia's neck, leaning against her when Leonita entered her, stroking that sweet spot inside her while she sucked her clit. The sounds of well-pleasured women filled the room, adding to the erotic atmosphere. Flavia's body tightened, her toes curled, and she reached a space where there was no thought, only colors and feelings.

She heard a frantic keening somewhere in the distance, dimly aware that it came from her own throat. She knew the orgasm was coming, but when it hit, the force nearly shattered her and her muscles contracted and shuddered for the next several minutes as she had several more. Her next awareness was of hands laying her down on the couch, then the weight of Leonita as she joined her. Flavia held onto her while she also continued to tremble.

It was a long while before she regained her senses. She opened her eyes to look at The Lioness. Leonita. The love she saw reflected in her eyes nearly broke her heart. How in the world was she going to let her go?

"Leonita?"

"Yes, love."

Flavia sighed when Leonita caressed her cheek. "I need a personal guard."

Leonita's eyes crinkled around the edges when she smiled back at her. "I'll take that position. It's too cold at the beach at this time of year anyway."

RECIPE FOR A ROMAN FEAST

Ingredients

Wine, lots of it

Erotic fruits, such as figs and wine-soaked pears

Oysters and an assortment of juicy meats

Several starving women

Directions

1. Combine all ingredients and blend until satiated.

2. Remove two women in love and let them continue feeding each other.

ABOUT THE AUTHORS

ASHLEY BARTLETT

Ashley Bartlett was born and raised in California. Her life consists of reading and writing. Most of the time, Ashley engages in these pursuits while sitting in front of a coffee shop with her girlfriend and smoking cigarettes. It's a glamorous life. She is an obnoxious, sarcastic, punk-ass, but her friends don't hold that against her.

She currently lives in Sacramento, but you can find her at www.ashbartlett.com.

JOVE BELLE

Jove Belle lives in Vancouver, Washington with her family. Her books include *The Job*, *Uncommon Romance*, *Love and Devotion*, *Indelible*, *Chaps*, *Split the Aces*, and *Edge of Darkness*.

To learn more about Jove, check her out online at www.jovebelle.com.

CHEYENNE BLUE

Cheyenne Blue's erotica has appeared in over 90 anthologies, including *Best Women's Erotica*, *Cowboy Lust*, *Best Lesbian Romance*, *Lesbian Lust*, and *Frenzy: 60 Stories of Sudden Sex*. She is editor of the upcoming anthology *Forbidden Fruit: stories of unwise lesbian desire*. Cheyenne lives and writes by the beach in Queensland, Australia.

Visit her website at www.cheyenneblue.com or find her on Twitter @iamcheyenneblue.

CHERI CRYSTAL

Cheri Crystal is a healthcare professional by day and writes erotic romances by night. She is a native New Yorker who was born in Brooklyn and raised on Long Island. Recently, Cheri has crossed the pond to live in the United Kingdom with her loving wife. A day doesn't go by that she doesn't miss her three kids, technically adults, but thanks to Skype and lots of visits with her family, she enjoys living on England's southwest coast. Cheri began writing fiction in 2003 after reviewing for Lambda Book Report, *Just About Write*, *Independent Gay Writer*, and other e-zines. She is the author of *Attractions of the Heart*, a 2010 Golden Crown Literary Winner for lesbian erotica. In her spare time, she enjoys swimming, hiking, viewing wildlife, cooking, jigsaw puzzles, and spending quality time with family and friends.

Visit her on the web at
www.chericrystal.com
www.facebook.com/chericrystal
and www.amazon.com/Cheri-Crystal/e/B002VG3738
for the latest news.

R.G. EMANUELLE

A New York City native, R.G. Emanuelle is the author of *Twice Bitten* and *Add Spice to Taste*, and has had stories published in numerous anthologies, including *Best Lesbian Erotica 2010*, *Women With Handcuffs*, and *When The Clock Strikes Thirteen*. She is co-editor of *Skulls and Crossbones: Tales of Women Pirates* from Bedazzled Ink and the forthcoming *Unwrap These Presents* from Ylva Publishing. When she's not writing or editing, she can usually be found cooking or developing recipes, as she is also a culinary school graduate.

You can find her at

www.rgemanuelle.com

www.facebook.com/RGEmanuelle

or Twitter @RGEmanuelle.

SACCHI GREEN

Sacchi Green is a writer and editor of erotica and other stimulating genres. Her stories have appeared in scores of publications, and she's also edited nine lesbian erotica anthologies, including Lambda Award winners *Lesbian Cowboys* and *Wild Girls, Wild Nights*, both from Cleis Press. A collection of her own work, *A Ride to Remember*, has been published by Lethe Press. Sacchi lives in western Massachusetts and gets away to the mountains of New Hampshire as often as she can.

http://sacchi-green.blogspot.com

YVONNE HEIDT

Yvonne Heidt currently lives in Texas with her partner of thirteen years, where she channels her inner rock star on Friday nights. Her first book, *Sometime Yesterday*, won the 2012 Golden Crown Literary Award for Best Paranormal Romance in addition to being a finalist in the Lambda

Literary Awards. She also won the 2013 Golden Crown Literary Award in paranormal fiction for her novel, *The Awakening.* While growing up, her mother constantly asked her, "Where do you come up with this stuff, Yvonne?"

The answer was—and is—always the same: "I don't know. I just make it up as I go along."

HISTORIA

Historia, an author living in New York City, writes stories of love from a time and place other than our own.

JAE

Jae grew up amidst the vineyards and gently sloping hills of southern Germany. She spent most of her childhood with her nose buried in a book, earning her the nickname "professor." The writing bug bit her at the age of eleven. For the last eight years, she has been writing mostly in English. She used to work as a psychologist but gave up her day job in December 2013 to become a full-time writer and a part-time editor. As far as she's concerned, she's got the best job in the world.

When she's not writing, she likes to spend her time reading, indulging her ice cream and office supply addictions, and watching way too many crime shows.

E-Mail: jae@jae-fiction.com

Website: http://jae-fiction.com

Facebook: www.facebook.com/JaeAuthor

ANDI MARQUETTE

Andi Marquette is an editor and award-winning author of mysteries, science fiction, and romance. Her latest novels include *Day of the Dead*, the Goldie-nominated *The Edge of Rebellion*, and *From the Hat Down*.

Find out more about her work at her website: www.andimarquette.com.

VICTORIA OLDHAM

Victoria Oldham is a full-time lesbian fiction editor and erotica writer. She lives in England with her partner and is often off gallivanting around Europe, when she isn't chained to her desk working. Her writing can be found in various anthologies, including *Women of the Dark Streets*, *She Shifters* and *Girls Who Bite*.

www.victoria-oldham.co.uk

KARIS WALSH

Karis Walsh is the author of several Bold Strokes Books romances, including Rainbow Award winning *Harmony* and *Sea Glass Inn*, a romantic intrigue called *Mounting Danger*, and multiple short stories. A Pacific Northwest native, she has recently moved to the great state of Texas, where she lives with her partner, various furry kids, and an overworked air conditioner. When not writing or soaking up the unfamiliar sunshine, she loves to read, cook spicy food, and play her viola or violin.

Visit her at www.kariswalsh.com or www.facebook.com/karis.walsh.7.

REBEKAH WEATHERSPOON

Rebekah Weatherspoon was raised in Southern New Hampshire and now lives in Southern California with her favorite human and their two furry babies. She writes steamy multicultural contemporary and paranormal romance, both New Adult and Adult.

You can find all of her titles at: www.rebekahweatherspoon.com.

OTHER BOOKS FROM YLVA PUBLISHING

http://www.ylva-publishing.com

DEPARTURE FROM THE SCRIPT

Jae

ISBN: 978-3-95533-195-5 (paperback)
Length: 240 pages

Aspiring actress Amanda Clark and photographer Michelle Osinski are two women burned by love and not looking to test the fire again. And even if they were, it certainly wouldn't be with each other.

Amanda has never been attracted to a butch woman before, and Michelle personifies the term butch. Having just landed a role on a hot new TV show, she's determined to focus on her career and doesn't need any complications in her life.

After a turbulent breakup with her starlet ex, Michelle swore she would never get involved with an actress again. Another high-maintenance woman is the last thing she wants, and her first encounter with Amanda certainly makes her appear the type.

But after a date that is not a date and some meddling from Amanda's grandmother, they both begin to wonder if it's not time for a departure from their usual dating scripts.

WHEN THE CLOCK STRIKES THIRTEEN

Lois Cloarec Hart, L.T. Smith, Emma Weimann, Joan Arling, Diane Marina, Erzabet Bishop, R.G. Emanuelle

ISBN: 978-3-95533-155-9 (paperback)
Length: 175 pages

Midnight Messages
Lois Cloarec Hart

Luce Sheppard can't ignore it any longer. She has to make a decision and time grows short. But refusing to make a decision is a decision, and she retires to bed, prepared to accept the results of her non-decision. That night an unexpected midnight visitor lands on her doorstep. Keira Keller, a distraught teenager, has lost her way home after a disastrous party. Luce steps in to help and in doing so receives answers to questions she didn't know she'd asked.

Batteries Not Included
L.T. Smith

Alex Stevens is a workaholic and a loner. Nothing and nobody can get past the cool exterior and solitary walls she has painstakingly created.

Until one night in October. One night that makes her step back and reassess what it means to be alive.

Lost and Found
Emma Weimann

Laura Sullivan flees to her grandparents' old cottage to escape the haunting memories of finding her brother in bed with her girlfriend. But even in rural Ireland, tranquility is easier to find than peace—especially when she meets an otherworldly being that leaves her a reminder she didn't count on.

Chrysalis
Joan Arling

Tara is a nice little girl. Her friends, on the other hand, are... peculiar... A breeze of a story. Or the other way 'round.

Sisters of the Moon
Diane Marina

The week before Halloween, Nicole joins her friends on a local ghost tour. In addition to visiting spooky sights and haunted grounds, she meets an enticing woman who makes her spine tingle. Who is the mysterious stranger? And how will the encounter end?

Wolf Moon
Erzabet Bishop

Seeking diversion from her job as a bookstore manager, Lindsay goes to a Halloween party at a convention center—and finds much more than she bargained for.

Werewolf Detective Taggert responds to a bomb threat at the convention center. An explosive situation, especially when raw chemistry hits them full force.

Can Lindsay open her heart and accept the fierce love of a red-hot shifter, or will they go their separate ways?

Love Bites
R.G. Emanuelle

New Orleans. Vampires. Jodi goes to the former and finds the latter. She feels a mysterious pull that leads her to The Big Easy and to freedom, passion, and the startling revelation of what having too many daiquiris can make her do.

COMING HOME
(revised edition)

Lois Cloarec Hart

ISBN: 978-3-95533-064-4 (paperback)
Length: 371 pages

A triangle with a twist, *Coming Home* is the story of three good people caught up in an impossible situation.

Rob, a charismatic ex-fighter pilot severely disabled with MS, has been steadfastly cared for by his wife, Jan, for many years. Quite by accident one day, Terry, a young writer/postal carrier, enters their lives and turns it upside down.

Injecting joy and turbulence into their quiet existence, Terry draws Rob and Jan into her lively circle of family and friends until the growing attachment between the two women begins to strain the bonds of love and loyalty, to Rob and each other.

IN A HEARTBEAT

RJ Nolan

ISBN: 978-3-95533-159-7 (paperback)
Length: 370 pages

Veteran police officer Sam McKenna has no trouble facing down criminals on a daily basis but breaks out in a sweat at the mere mention of commitment. A recent failed relationship strengthens her resolve to stick with her trademark no-strings-attached affairs.

Dr. Riley Connolly, a successful trauma surgeon, has spent her whole life trying to measure up to her family's expectations. And that includes hiding her sexuality from them.

When a routine call sends Sam to the hospital where Riley works, the two women are hurtled into a life-and-death situation. The incident binds them together. But can there be any future for a commitment-phobic cop and a closeted, workaholic doctor?

HEART'S SURRENDER

Emma Weimann

ISBN: 978-3-95533-183-2 (paperback)
Length: 305 pages

Neither Samantha Freedman nor Gillian Jennings are looking for a relationship when they begin a no-strings-attached affair. But soon simple attraction turns into something more.

What happens when the worlds of a handywoman and a pampered housewife collide? Can nights of hot, erotic fun lead to love, or will these two very different women go their separate ways?

COMING FROM YLVA PUBLISHING IN FALL 2014

http://www.ylva-publishing.com

STILL LIFE

L.T. Smith

After breaking off her relationship with a female lothario, Jess Taylor decides she doesn't want to expose herself to another cheating partner. Staying at home, alone, suits her just fine. Her idea of a good night is an early one—preferably with a good book. Well, until her best friend, Sophie Harrison, decides it's time Jess rejoined the human race.

Trying to pull Jess from her self-imposed prison, Sophie signs them both up for a Still Life art class at the local college. Sophie knows the beautiful art teacher, Diana Sullivan, could be the woman her best friend needs to move on with her life.

But, in reality, could art bring these two women together? Could it be strong enough to make a masterpiece in just twelve sessions? And, more importantly, can Jess overcome her fear of being used once again?

Only time will tell.

BARRING COMPLICATIONS

Blythe Rippon

It's an open secret that the newest justice on the Supreme Court is a lesbian. So when the Court decides to hear a case about gay marriage, Justice Victoria Willoughby must navigate the press, sway at least one of her conservative colleagues, and confront her own fraught feelings about coming out.

Just when she decides she's up to the challenge, she learns that the very brilliant, very out Genevieve Fornier will be lead counsel on the case.

Genevieve isn't sure which is causing her more sleepless nights: the prospect of losing the case, or the thought of who will be sitting on the bench when she argues it.

THE RETURN

Ana Matics

Near Haven is like any other small, dying fishing village dotting the Maine coastline—a crusty remnant of an industry long gone, a place that is mired in sadness and longing for what was and can never be again. People move away, yet they always seem to come back. It's a vicious cycle of small-town America.

Liza Hawke thought that she'd gotten out, escaped across the country on a basketball scholarship. A series of bad decisions, however, has her returning home after nearly a decade. She struggles to accept her place in the fabric of this small coastal town, making amends to the people she's wronged and trying to rebuild her life in the process.

Her return marks the beginning of a shift within the town as the residents that she's hurt so badly start to heal once more.

ISBN (paperback): 978-3-95533-224-2

The title is also available as an ebook.

Published by Ylva Publishing, legal entity of Ylva Verlag, e.Kfr.

Ylva Verlag, e.Kfr.
Owner: Astrid Ohletz
Am Kirschgarten 2
65830 Kriftel
Germany

http://www.ylva-publishing.com

First edition: August 2014

Cover photo © Bigstock.com/"Carhop" by rformidable
Cover design by Sue Niewiarowski, n-design.com
TOC design/layout by R.G. Emanuelle
Interior text design by Streetlight Graphics

CPSIA information can be obtained
at www.ICGtesting.com
Printed in the USA
FFOW04n2243010415
12335FF